Cover design by: Getcover

CONTENTS

TRIGGER WARNING

This book contains dark themes that may be distressing to some readers. These include: abduction and captivity, emotionally and physically manipulative relationships, sexual situations with power imbalances, emotionally intense and explicit sexual content, scenes of violence and torture, death, grief, and psychological trauma.

Please read with care and check content warnings if you have sensitivities.

If you've made it this far... welcome to the dark side, where the shadow daddies play for keeps.

HELLS BLESSED

BOOK THREE
IN THE BLESSED SERIES

KAY HUGHES

PROLOGUE

Raya & Rhadis - Ages Eleven & Twelve

The light is soft, slipping through the trees in broken patches, and the lake ahead shimmers in ripples under the afternoon sun. I dig my heels into the cool earth beside the water, letting the edge of my toe dip into the lake. My reflection wavers with the gentle breeze, and I reach a hand out as if I can capture it. Rhadis sits beside me, a twig in his hand, lazily tracing patterns into the sand. He's only twelve, but already he has a quiet, watchful stillness I've come to recognize as a part of him, as though he's more at home observing than acting. Still, when he does speak, it's like he's giving away a secret.

"Do you think there are Foxes in those woods?" I ask, pointing to the far edge of the lake where the trees grow dense and dark, blending into shadows. I know they're there, even if I haven't seen them—Foxes, Tencans, maybe even aWolfer, all hidden from us but close.

He nods, following my gaze with a thoughtful expression. "I've seen them before. Once, I even got close enough to see one up close."

My eyes widen. "Really? Were you scared?"

He grins, his dark hair falling messily across his forehead. "No. They're smart. They only attack if they feel threatened."

I tilt my head, studying him, imagining the courage it must have taken to stand so close to something wild. "You're lucky, Rhadis. I'd like to see them up close too. But not the Wolfers," I add quickly. "They're too big."

He leans back, propping his elbows on the grass, looking at me as though the woods, the lake, and all its mysteries are nothing to worry about. "One day, maybe I'll take you to see them. All of them. Even the Wolfers."

The idea fills me with a strange mix of excitement and fear, and I look down, kicking at a small pebble near my foot. "But… What if something happens? What if… What if they come too close? Or they want to eat me?"

He sits up a little straighter, watching me carefully. "Then I'll be there," he says, his voice steady. "I'll protect you, Raya. No matter what."

There's a seriousness to his words that makes me pause, as though he's telling me something he wants me to remember long after today. I lift my chin, meeting his eyes, trying to hold on to that feeling, to the way he says it like it's a promise.

"But what about later?" I ask, dropping my voice, my fingers digging into the grass. "When you're older, and… And they call you away? Won't you have to leave these lands? To become what you're supposed to be?"

His smile fades, and for a moment, there's a sadness in his eyes, like he's already thought of this before. But then he shakes his head, almost stubbornly. "No. I won't leave you, Raya."

I study him, trying to understand what he's really saying. "Not ever?"

He hesitates, his gaze steady on mine, and in that moment, I want so badly to believe him. "I'll protect you," he repeats softly, as though saying it a second time will make it true. "No matter where I go, or what happens. I promise."

My heart feels strangely full, and I reach out, brushing a strand of hair from my face as I stare at him. "You really mean it?"

"Yes," he says, without hesitation, the certainty in his voice warming something deep inside me. "I'll always keep you safe, Raya. Forever, I promise."

A quiet smile spreads across my face, and I reach for his hand, gripping it tightly. We sit like that in the silence, the promise hanging between us, something unbreakable. It's a moment so simple, so precious, that it feels as though it's ours alone, hidden in the shelter of the trees and the soft rustle of the lake, sealed like a secret we'll keep safe for the rest of our lives.

CHAPTER ONE

I make my way down the dimly lit corridor, my mind racing with everything that's happened, everything that's been said. Rhadis, standing there so smug, telling me I'll be staying in his cot Not even asking—just telling me as if I'm some part of his decor that he can arrange however he likes. As if I was his servant.

How dare he? And how dare he still have this effect on me?

My fists clench and unclench as I walk. I should be focused on Emory, on everything we're facing with Ymir, but my thoughts circle back to Rhadis like some kind of curse I can't escape. It's maddening. After all these years, the memory of his smile from when we were children—the easy, warm smile he had back then—still haunts me. And now, I barely recognize him. There's a hardness in his eyes, a sharp edge that wasn't there before, and yet somehow, I find myself caught, wondering if that boy I knew is still in there somewhere.

I don't want to admit how much it's shaken me seeing him again. I tell myself it's nothing, just the shock of the reunion. But deep down, I know it's not that simple. Feelings I buried long ago seem to have resurfaced, clawing their way back to the surface, no matter how I try to shove them down.

I take a steadying breath, my footsteps slowing as I approach the heavy wooden door he pointed out. The shadows dance along the walls, casting everything in an eerie glow, and I hesitate for a moment, hand hovering over the handle. My heart is beating faster than it should, and I can't stand that he has me feeling this way. I'm angry, yes—but beneath it all, I know there's more to it, and that makes me even angrier.

Finally, I push open the door. The room is larger than I expected, a blend of dark, luxurious fabrics and old, heavy wood. Dark curtains drape from the windows, the walls lined with shelves and strange trinkets I don't recognize. Everything in here is distinctly him, an extension of the mysterious, powerful god he's become.

And then there's the cot.

It sits against the far wall, enormous and inviting, covered in deep blue and gold furs, a stark contrast to the muted tones of the rest of the room. The thought of sharing it with him makes my heart pound, though I'd never admit that to anyone. I know I'm supposed to be furious with him, and I am—but there's an excitement, too, something I can't quite name.

I walk farther into the room, glancing around at the subtle hints of the person he's become. There's a worn leather-bound book on one of the tables, a half-full glass of something dark on another. I can't help but wonder if he spends his nights alone here, wandering through whatever darkness fills his mind. He was always drawn to the shadows, even as a child, but now… it's like he's become part of them.

As I stand there, I feel a strange mix of anticipation and fear. I've spent so long thinking of him as my childhood friend, the one person who could make me laugh even when the world felt too heavy. But that boy is gone, replaced by this man I barely know.

And yet, a part of me still wants to know him.

But I can't get lost in him again. I remind myself of Emory, of why we're all here in the first place. There's so much at stake, so many battles ahead, and I need to keep my focus. Rhadis… he's a distraction I can't afford. And yet, as I sit on the edge of that cot, feeling the weight of it beneath me, I can't help but think that maybe, just maybe, he's exactly the distraction I want.

I look up sharply as the door opens, my pulse quickening at the sight of Rhadis filling the doorway. His gaze is steady, unreadable as it sweeps over me, lingering just long enough to make me shift under its weight. He closes the door behind him, a smirk pulling at the corner of his mouth.

"Well," he says, his voice low, "is it to your liking, Raya?"

I hate the casual confidence in his tone, as if he knows exactly what he's doing by throwing me off balance. The years may have changed us both, but he still knows how to rile me up with just a look. I straighten my shoulders, determined not to let him see any hint of my hesitation.

"It's… fine," I say, trying to keep my voice neutral. "Although you didn't give me much choice in the matter, did you?"

His smirk deepens, and he crosses his arms, leaning against the doorframe with an ease that only irritates me more. "No, I didn't," he replies smoothly. "But if I had, would you have chosen differently?"

I scoff, looking away from him as I try to regain some semblance of control. "I would have at least chosen a cot I didn't have to share with you."

Rhadis chuckles, a low sound that echoes through the room, and I can feel the heat rising in my cheeks despite my best efforts. "Come now, Raya. After everything we've been through, sharing a bed is the least of our worries."

His words catch me off guard, and for a moment, a flicker of the past—the warmth of his smile, the laughter we used to share—passes between us. But then it's gone, replaced by that familiar, infuriating glint in his eyes. I feel a surge of anger mixed with something I refuse to name.

"So this is just a game to you, then?" I ask, trying to sound indifferent, but the frustration slips into my voice. "Playing house while the rest of us are here fighting for our lives?"

Rhadis's expression shifts, the amusement in his eyes dimming. He steps closer, the air thickening as he closes the distance between us. "You think this is a game?" His voice is quieter now, edged with something serious, something darker. "Raya, I brought you here because it's the safest place for you all. The last thing I'd ever do is put you in danger."

I don't know how to respond to that, the intensity in his gaze stealing the words from me. For a moment, we just stand there, the silence settling over us like a weight, each of us unwilling to break it. My heart races, and I can feel his presence in every inch of the room, closing in around me.

Finally, I manage to find my voice, though it sounds quieter than I intended. "Why me, Rhadis? Why make me stay here, in your room?"

His gaze softens, just a fraction, and for the first time, I see a glimpse of vulnerability beneath the hard exterior he wears like armor. "Because I don't want you anywhere else," he says, his voice barely above a whisper.

The words hang between us, heavy and raw, and I feel something shift inside me, something I've tried to bury for years. I want to push him away, to shield myself from whatever this is between us, but instead, I find myself holding my ground, unable to look away.

After a beat, he lets out a breath, almost as if he hadn't meant to say that out loud. "I'll leave you to settle in," he murmurs, turning to the door. But before he leaves, he pauses, glancing back over his shoulder. "If you need anything, Raya... just call for me."

And with that, he's gone, the door clicking shut behind him, leaving me alone with the echo of his words and the relentless pounding of my heart.

CHAPTER TWO

I settle onto the edge of the oversized cot, its dark blue furs thick and rich beneath my hands. Rhadis's words from earlier linger in my mind, weaving themselves around memories I'd tried to keep locked away. *"I'll protect you, Raya. No matter what."*

The promise he made so many years ago echoes, and I can't help but wonder if he even remembers saying it. I can't let myself believe it—not after all these years, after all the changes in him that I don't understand.

I glance around, hoping to find something to distract myself. His room is surprisingly neat, more organized than I expected for someone as unpredictable as Rhadis. Tall shelves line one wall, filled with a collection of books, artifacts, and trinkets. They're arranged meticulously, almost like each item holds a specific purpose, a piece of a puzzle only he knows how to solve. There's a small, carved wooden box on the edge of one shelf, intricate patterns etched into the dark wood. I reach out, my fingers hovering over it before I pick it up, turning it over in my hands.

The box is heavier than I expected, its craftsmanship delicate and intentional. I lift the lid, expecting to see something valuable or strange, but inside there's only a small piece of cloth, folded carefully. I run my fingers over it, the material soft and worn with age. It looks like it once belonged to a child—a fragment of something he's kept all this time. For a second, a warmth spreads through me, a curiosity about what this small white piece of fabric might mean to him.

Setting the box down, I move on, pulling open a drawer built into the base of the shelf. Inside, I find a stack of papers, maps layered with notes in his careful handwriting. Some are old, the edges fraying, while others look freshly drawn, marked with arrows and symbols I can't quite decipher. There are notes about the realms, the barriers between them, scribbles that seem to trace the movements of people… people he's been watching.

One name catches my eye, written boldly in the center of a page: *Emory*. My heart skips, and I realize that he's been tracking her, mapping her path since she left. The realization feels both comforting and strange, knowing he's kept such a close watch, even when he said he wanted no part in this war. I wonder if he's been doing the same for me, tracing my steps in his own way.

I close the drawer, moving to the small table near the cot. A single half burned candle sits atop it, and beside it, a leather-bound journal. My fingers itch to open it, but I hesitate, feeling a little guilty. This is his private space, his sanctuary—and yet, the temptation is too strong. But, he did invite me, no, force me, into this space. I flip it open, glancing at the handwriting that fills the page. The words are written in neat, precise lines, each entry short and to the point.

One entry catches my attention, the date back to when I was around seventeen. Long after he had gone: *"Saw her today by the lake. The same lake where I promised to protect her forever. She's grown, but she hasn't changed."*

I can almost hear his voice in the words, and a warmth spreads through me before I quickly shut the journal, my pulse racing. I stand there for a moment, just breathing, as though the room holds a part of him I didn't expect to see—a part of him that still remembers, even if he hides it behind walls of stone.

I step away from the table, taking in the room with new eyes, wondering what else he's kept hidden here. Every corner seems to carry a piece of him, a mystery waiting to be uncovered.

I settle into my search, slipping from one corner of the room to another, finding little glimpses of Rhadis in the things he's chosen to keep. It feels strange, intimate even, being surrounded by all these pieces of him when he isn't here to see it. Part of me knows I shouldn't be snooping like this—but I can't stop. I want to know him, the way he is now, the parts of him he doesn't show, the secrets he keeps hidden.

I slide open the small wardrobe beside his cot, and it's as organized as everything else, with shirts and tunics folded neatly. I pull one out, the fabric heavier than I expected, brushed with faint embroidery along the collar. It smells faintly of him—a scent that's familiar, woodsy and warm. The scent tugs at something in me, a memory that slips away before I can catch it. Carefully, I fold the shirt back, tucking it away as if I hadn't been here at all.

Next, I move to his bookshelf. The titles are varied, some familiar and others written in languages I don't understand. One book catches my eye: a thick volume with faded gold lettering along the spine. When I pull it out, a small slip of paper flutters to the ground. I pick it up, noticing it's a simple note, the edges worn as though it's been handled too many times. The handwriting is different from his—it's delicate, with words of thanks written in soft strokes. I turn it over, wondering who could have given this to him and why he's kept it. There's no name, just a few lines, but it's enough to stir questions that linger as I slide the note back into place.

On a shelf higher up, I find a carved stone figure, small enough to fit in the palm of my hand. It's rough, unfinished, a shape that resembles a bird in flight. The detail is crude, as though it was made by someone with little practice, but there's something earnest about it. A quiet smile tugs at my lips as I turn the small carving over in my hands, remembering him as a boy, when he had always picked up new hobbies to pass his time. When I place it back, I can almost see him beside me, laughing at my curiosity.

A few hours have passed as I ruffled through his books and clothing and I now make my way to the adjoining bathing chamber. I half-expect it to be as sparse and orderly as the rest of the room, but it's... surprisingly personal. I step into the bathing chamber, and the air shifts around me, heavy with the scent of cedar, vanilla, and something warm and earthy. The room feels like a secret haven, a place carved out from the world. It's grand but not overwhelming, the kind of space that demands reverence without shouting its importance.

The tub catches my eye first. It's massive, made of polished black marble, so smooth it almost seems to pulse with its own quiet energy. The water inside shimmers, a deep, inviting pool that reflects the soft, flickering light from the candles scattered around the room. From the edge of the tub, a small fountain pours water, the gentle sound of it filling the silence with a rhythmic, soothing splash.

I step closer, my feet sinking into the coolness of the delicate green and gold tiles that line the floor. The patterns swirl beneath me, each tile a perfect piece of a larger, more intricate design. My steps feel deliberate here, as though the floor itself is guiding me into the space. I can almost feel the weight of the room, pressing in on me, and yet it's calming—an embrace rather than a confinement.

The walls are painted in a soft, sage color, like the first hint of dawn. They seem to breathe with the room, their calm shade making the space feel open and restful. I turn slightly, and my gaze lands on the marble countertop beside the tub. It's lined with an assortment of razors, their sharp blades glinting in the candlelight, a few bars of soap stacked neatly beside them. The soaps are wrapped in delicate parchment, each one a different shade, their scents mixing together in a warm, inviting blend. There's something grounding about the whole scene—each element perfectly placed, like it's waiting for me to take my time, to indulge in the ritual of it all.

I pause for a moment, letting the stillness of the room settle around me, before I take another step toward the tub. The water looks so inviting, so warm, and for a second, I forget where I am, lost in the quiet beauty of the space. I take a deep breath, inhaling the rich scent of the air, and let the tension in my shoulders begin to melt away.

I can't help but feel his presence in this space, even though he's not here. There's something about it—the way everything is arranged, the soft gleam of the marble, the steady trickle of the fountain—that speaks of him. Of his power. His care. His attention to every detail.

And yet, it's strangely peaceful here, too. Something about the stillness makes me feel like time has paused, just for me. I walk closer to the tub, the flickering light of the candles dancing across the water, and wonder what it would feel like to sink into its warmth, to let it wash away everything outside these walls.

There are soft towels folded neatly on a shelf, but I notice one in particular—it's worn and frayed, as though he's held onto it for too long. Beside it, there's a small collection of polished stones, smoothed by water, tucked into a ceramic dish. I run my fingers over them, feeling the coolness beneath my touch. They're simple, small stones, the kind you'd pick up by the shore, yet he's kept them as though they mean something to him.

There's a glass bottle on the edge of the basin, filled with a fragrant oil I recognize—lavender and cedar, grounding and earthy. I breathe it in, my shoulders relaxing as the scent fills the space. It's clear he uses it often, the bottle half-empty. I can picture him here, winding down after a long day, this scent filling the air around him.

I find myself smiling as I leave the bathing chamber, a warmth blooming in my chest. Despite the years, despite the distance and the walls he's built, there are small parts of him that feel unchanged, pieces of the boy I knew woven through everything he's chosen to keep. These little fragments tell me more about him than his guarded words ever could.

As I step back into the room, my heart nearly stops. Rhadis is there, leaning casually against the wall, his arms crossed over his chest, watching me with that infuriatingly unreadable look in his eyes.

"How's the snooping been?" he asks, one brow lifting in mock curiosity.

Heat floods my cheeks, and I fight the instinct to turn away. I've been caught. Completely, shamelessly caught. But the smirk he's wearing and the light in his eyes tell me he's more amused than angry.

"Just getting acquainted with my new… accommodations," I say, trying to muster whatever dignity I have left. "Wouldn't want to feel like a stranger in my own room, after all."

"Your own room, hmm?" He pushes off the wall and steps closer, closing the space between us until he's right there, his shadow wrapping around me. "And what interesting findings have you uncovered?"

I swallow, the air around us thick. He's not going to let me brush this off. "Nothing… too interesting," I reply, though I know it's a weak excuse. "A few books, some… stones. Thought you'd be more of a weapons and armor sort."

His gaze flickers, a glimmer of something softer passing over his features. "I have those too, don't worry," he says, voice low. "But it's good to know you're thorough."

I straighten my spine, tilting my chin up to meet his gaze. "And what would you have me do, Rhadis? Sit in a room full of your things and pretend they don't tell me something about you?"

He chuckles softly, brushing a stray lock of hair from my face. "I'd expect nothing less," he murmurs. His fingers linger a moment too long, and I can feel the warmth of his touch.

I clear my throat, searching for something to say to break the tension. "And what would you do if I said I'd found something... embarrassing?"

His smirk widens. "Then I'd remind you that you have a much longer stay ahead of you, and I can always find something equally embarrassing about you."

I roll my eyes, but my heart is racing. "I don't know, Rhadis. I think I have you well outmatched on the secret-keeping front."

"Oh?" His voice softens, taking on a darker edge. "Perhaps one day, you'll be brave enough to share some of those secrets with me."

The challenge in his words hangs in the air, heavy and unspoken. It feels like a dare, but there's an invitation there, too—a small glimpse that, underneath all his layers and armor, he wants to know me just as much as I want to understand him.

Rhadis gives me a small nod and gestures to the door, his tone shifting to something less teasing. "It's time for lunch," he says, as if that's all there is to say, like we're suddenly back to business as usual. He turns and strides toward the door, leaving me no choice but to follow.

The dining room is grand, with high windows and tapestries that sweep from ceiling to floor. Everything about this place, from the walls to the smallest decoration, speaks of someone with an eye for details that matter—someone meticulous. He pauses by the head of the table, waiting until I approach. I expect him to sit first, but instead, he pulls out the chair to his immediate right and motions for me to sit. His hand lingers for a moment as he pushes my chair in.

"Comfortable?" he asks, a hint of that smirk resurfacing as he takes his own seat.

I nod, feeling strangely out of place. But before I can lose myself in the discomfort of sitting next to him, he reaches for a parchment resting beside his plate. He unrolls it, eyes scanning over it with casual focus, and I can't help but lean closer to see.

It's a news report, columns filled with recent updates on the blights that have been creeping into the lands—their relentless spread, the villages affected, the rising fears. The stark descriptions capture my attention, and a chill pricks along my spine as I read about the damages. Blackened fields, livestock fallen ill, once-thriving villages slowly deserted. Rhadis doesn't seem fazed, but I sense a subtle tension in him.

"Any thoughts?" he murmurs, not looking up, though he knows

I'm reading alongside him.

"It's... tragic," I say quietly, not sure what else to say. The blights are spreading faster than we imagined. "Have the gifted found out that the war is the cause?"

He glances over at me, his expression hard to read. "No, though it is highly speculated. The gods claim they're investigating, but the truth is, most realms are left to fend for themselves."

His words are calm, but there's a bitterness beneath them, one that makes me realize just how much more Rhadis sees and knows than he lets on.

"Do you believe it will reach here?" I ask, my voice barely above a whisper. I can hardly believe I'm saying "here" like this place is my own home.

Rhadis pauses, folding the parchment with careful fingers. "It's highly unlikely, for now. The blights are—drawn to different life forms." He hesitates, meeting my eyes. "There are very few living within my realm. But that doesn't mean we're completely safe from the effects."

Just then, the servants come in, placing dishes on the table with the usual practiced quietness. I barely notice the fine dishware they've brought, my mind still on the words Rhadis has just spoken. He's watching me closely now, and I realize he's still holding that invitation, just like before.

It's an invitation to ask more, to understand more, and maybe to edge closer into the parts of him he never shows anyone else. But before I can utter another sentence, the rest of my friends are bustling into the room and taking their places around the table.

CHAPTER THREE

As I sit at the dining table, the room filled with the hum of conversation and the warmth of laughter, my attention drifts to Emory. She's leaning slightly forward, her eyes wide with wonder as our friends share stories of her past—memories that had been stolen from her, piece by piece. Each tale brings a little light back to her face, a spark of recognition or, at the very least, belonging.

"I remember when you challenged Haven to a race," Hellion says with a grin, his red hair catching the light as he leans back in his chair. "You are half her size, but you ran like the wind. And somehow, most likely because you forbade her from shifting, you won."

Emory laughs, her hand resting protectively over her belly as she shakes her head. "That doesn't sound like me," she says, her voice full of soft disbelief.

"Oh, it was you," Eira chimes in, her pale blue dress fluttering as she gestures animatedly. "And you were smug about it for weeks. It drove everyone mad."

The laughter around the table deepens, and I find myself smiling, too, even as my thoughts begin to wander. The stories being shared bring a warmth to the room, but they also remind me of my own memories—ones I would rather forget.

My hand tightens slightly around the edge of the table as my mind slips backward, drawn to the dark corners of my childhood. To the day I was stolen from my home.

I was just a child, no older than eight, when the Arrakis soldiers came. My home was warm and safe—small but filled with love, with the smell of my mother's cooking and my father's quiet strength. And then it was gone. They came in the night, their voices harsh and foreign, tearing me from the only life I had ever known.

The war ground they brought me to was nothing like home. It was a bleak, brutal place meant to break children like me, to shape them into servants or soldiers for the gods and lords who ruled these lands. I was too small, too weak to fight, so they made me a servant. A maid to clean the boots of warriors and scrub the halls of their homesteads. I remember the constant hunger, the gnawing ache in my stomach that never seemed to go away. The bruises from impatient hands when I didn't move fast enough. The cold floor I slept on at night, huddled in the corner, afraid to close my eyes for too long.

And then there was Rhadis.

He wasn't like the others. He was brought there to train for something greater, something darker—to prepare him for the underworld he was destined to rule. But despite that, he saw me.

He noticed me. While the others ignored me or treated me like I was nothing, Rhadis would talk to me, offer me food when no one was looking, even share a smile that felt like the only light in that bleak place.

For a time, he was the only good thing I had. He didn't judge me for being small or scared, didn't see me as just another servant. He saw me as Raya.

But even that was short-lived. After a few years, he was taken away, sent somewhere else to continue his training. I didn't understand why at the time—I just knew that he was gone, and I was alone again. Alone to face the beatings when I faltered, the nights of hunger that stretched endlessly. Without him, the days blurred into each other, a never-ending cycle of pain and survival until I was rescued by Dyra, the God of Love.

"Raya?" Emory's voice pulls me back to the present, her soft, concerned tone cutting through the fog of my memories.

I blink, realizing that everyone is looking at me. The warmth of the room feels distant now, like I've been dropped back into the cold shadows of the past.

"Sorry," I say quickly, forcing a smile. "I must have drifted off. What were you saying?"

Emory tilts her head, studying me with those sharp, curious eyes of hers, but she doesn't press. "Just another story," she says gently. "You've heard enough of mine. Maybe next time, you'll share one of yours."

I smile again, though it feels weaker this time. "Maybe," I

murmur, but my chest tightens at the thought. There are stories I could share, but none of them are the kind that would bring laughter to the table.

As the conversation picks up again, I steal a glance at Rhadis, seated at the head of the table. He's listening quietly, his dark eyes focused on the others, but I wonder if he feels my gaze. If he remembers the years we spent together at that war ground. If he remembers the promises he made to me and the girl I was back then.

Because I remember. Even now, I remember. And no matter how much time has passed, I wonder if the boy I knew is still in there somewhere—or if he's been lost to the man he's become and the things he has been forced to do while ruling the underworld.

The dining room clears slowly, the air heavy with the quiet contentment of a meal well enjoyed. Chairs scrape against the polished floors as everyone rises, murmuring soft goodbyes or excuses to return to their rooms. I stay seated, my hands resting on the smooth wood of the table, watching as Emory follows Ryat out, her hand resting protectively over her belly. The others follow in pairs or groups, their voices fading into the hallways.

I'm just beginning to consider doing the same when Rhadis stands from his chair and approaches me, his steps silent but certain. He pauses beside my chair, his dark eyes unreadable as he gazes down at me.

"Would you like to go somewhere with me?" he asks, his voice low but filled with that quiet intensity that always unsettles me.

I tilt my head, feeling wary. "Where?"

He doesn't answer immediately. Instead, his lips curl into the faintest hint of a smile, one that's almost teasing but too mysterious to be comforting. "Do you trust me?" he asks instead, his voice steady, as if the answer doesn't matter to him, though his eyes say otherwise.

The question hangs in the air, weighty and deliberate. Trust. It's a dangerous word when it comes to Rhadis, tangled in memories of the boy I knew and the man I don't. But there's something about the way he asks—soft, almost vulnerable—that makes me nod before I can overthink it.

"I… yes," I say, though my voice feels quieter than I intended.

That faint smile deepens just enough to spark a flicker of warmth in his eyes. "Then hold still," he murmurs.

Before I can ask what he means, his hand brushes my arm, and the world shifts beneath me. My breath catches as a swirling sensation overtakes me, the ground dissolving into a soft, shadowy pull. It's dark, but not harsh—more like velvet folding around me, cool and strangely gentle. There's power here, undeniable, but it doesn't scare me. It feels like a piece of Rhadis himself, dark and enigmatic but not cruel.

The sensation lasts only a moment before my feet find solid ground again. I blink, trying to adjust, and when I do, I realize we're outside.

The air is fresh, tinged with the earthy scent of moss and damp stone. A winding stone path stretches ahead of us, lined with soft, glowing fungi that cast a pale light as the sun lowers. The sky above is streaked with bright colors, painting the world in hues of gold and violet. The mountains loom tall and silent around us, their craggy faces softened by the shadows of dusk.

“Where are we?” I ask, my voice hushed in awe.

“You’ll see,” Rhadis replies, his tone quiet but filled with a strange kind of reverence. He gestures for me to follow, and I do, my footsteps echoing faintly on the stone path as we descend.

The air grows cooler as we approach the mouth of a cave, its wide entrance framed by hanging ivy and glittering minerals embedded in the stone. Inside, the air changes, carrying a soft humidity that clings to my skin. The faint sound of water reaches my ears—a gentle lapping, rhythmic and calming.

Rhadis steps aside, letting me pass him as the cave opens into a vast chamber. I gasp, my eyes widening at the sight before me.

A lake stretches out in the center of the cavern, its waters a soft, shimmering pink that reflects the faint light filtering in through cracks in the stone above. The glow isn’t harsh; it’s delicate, like the blush of dawn, and it dances across the ceiling in rippling patterns. Small fish dart through the water, their scales catching the light in flashes of silver and gold. The edges of the lake are lined with smooth stones and sand, and the scent of the water is faintly sweet, like blooming flowers.

“Rhadis…” I whisper, stepping forward, unable to tear my eyes away. The beauty of the place feels otherworldly, like something pulled from a dream.

He watches me closely, leaning against the stone wall with an ease that belies the effort it must have taken to bring us here. "This is a safe place within the underworld," he says simply, his voice echoing softly in the cavern. "I come here when I need to think. It's... quiet."

I kneel by the water's edge, my fingers skimming the surface. It's warm, like the perfect bath, and the ripples spread out in soft rings. "It's beautiful," I murmur, turning to look at him. "How did you know about this?"

"I didn't," he admits. "It's always been here. A part of this place. I found it when I was younger, during my training."

The mention of his training tugs at my chest, stirring memories I've tried to keep buried. I stand slowly, turning to face him fully. "Why did you bring me here?"

His gaze softens, the sharp edges of his usual demeanor fading. "Because I thought you might need it. A moment to breathe. To escape."

His words settle over me like a soft fur, and for the first time in what feels like ages, I let myself relax. The weight of everything —the war, Emory, even him—feels lighter here. I close my eyes, breathing in the air, and for a moment, I almost forget the world outside this cave exists.

Rhadis steps closer, his quiet movements stirring the still air of the cavern. His presence is steady, commanding, and as his hand brushes my arm, I shiver—not from the coolness of the cave, but from the touch itself. He gently tucks a stray strand of hair behind my ear, his fingers lingering for just a moment longer than necessary.

"We should swim," he says softly, his deep voice echoing faintly in the open space.

I glance at the water, at the way it shimmers in soft pinks and golds. "I... I don't have a swimsuit," I say awkwardly, my hands instinctively brushing over my sides, as if that might somehow solve the problem.

Rhadis chuckles, the sound low and rich, and he starts unbuttoning his shirt without another word. My breath catches as I realize what he's doing, and I force myself to keep my eyes on his face. But his movements are deliberate, methodical, and I can't help but notice the way his broad shoulders and chest come into view as he shrugs off the dark fabric. His skin is marked by scars, some small and faded, others deep and jagged. Some I recognize, memories flashing of times I'd seen him hurt, my small hands bandaging wounds I thought were too deep to heal. But there are others—newer ones I can't place, evidence of battles fought long after he left.

Rhadis doesn't stop. He pulls off his boots, his pants following, until he stands before me, entirely bare. I don't mean to stare, but I can't look away. His body is both familiar and foreign, every line and scar telling a story I haven't heard. The dim light of the cavern catches on his dark skin, highlighting the muscles beneath, and for a moment, I forget how to breathe.

He steps into the lake, the water rippling around him as he wades in, his movements graceful and unhurried. When he turns back to look at me, his gaze is steady, his lips quirking into that familiar, teasing smile.

"Are you just going to stand there staring, or are you going to join me?" he asks, his tone light but edged with something that feels like a challenge.

Heat floods my cheeks, and I quickly turn away. "Fine," I mutter, untying my boots and kicking them off, my fingers fumbling with the ties of my corset. My heart races as I undress, the weight of his gaze heavy on my back. I know he's watching, and though I try to block it out, I can feel his eyes trailing over me, studying me in that way he always has—like he's trying to figure me out.

When I step out of my dress, I hesitate. My arms cross over my chest instinctively, trying to shield myself as I approach the water. The cool stone beneath my feet shifts to smooth sand as I step in, the warmth of the lake surprising me as it laps at my ankles. I take another step, and then another, the water rising up to my thighs, my stomach, until it hides me completely.

I glance up, and Rhadis is still watching me, his dark eyes unwavering. His expression is unreadable, but there's something in the way he looks at me—something that makes me feel exposed, even beneath the cover of the water.

"You're tense," he says, his voice softer now, less teasing.

I let out a shaky breath, trying to relax. "It's not everyday someone drags me to a lake and—" I glance at him, biting back a nervous laugh. "And swims with me like this."

He grins, the scar on his lip pulling slightly. "I figured you could use something out of the ordinary."

The warmth of the water, the soft glow of the cavern, and

the steady presence of Rhadis begin to soothe me, though I'm acutely aware of every move I make, every glance he throws my way. As he swims closer, his movements slow and deliberate, I wonder what this moment means—why he brought me here, and why I let him.

Rhadis swims closer still, the water rippling gently around him, the soft pink hues catching the edges of his sharp features. My breath hitches as he stops just in front of me, his arms bracing on either side of a large, smooth stone behind me. I feel the coolness of the rock press against my back, and the contrasting warmth of his body fills the small space between us, making the water around us feel even hotter.

His dark eyes lock onto mine, and the faint red ring around his pupils seems to glow, casting an almost otherworldly light in the dim cavern. I can't look away, even though my heart is pounding so loudly in my chest I'm sure he can hear it. The air feels heavier here, like every breath is weighted with something unspoken.

"How does the water feel?" he asks, his voice low and intimate, the kind of tone that sends a shiver down my spine. It's as though the words are meant for me and me alone, echoing softly in the cavern but landing directly in my chest.

I swallow, trying to steady my voice. "It's… warm," I manage to say, though the heat blossoming in my core has nothing to do with the lake.

His lips quirk into a faint smirk, his gaze unwavering. "Good," he murmurs, his tone carrying a depth that makes me wonder if he's talking about more than just the water. His proximity is overwhelming—every movement, every breath he takes seems amplified. I can feel the heat radiating from his skin, even with the water between us, and it pulls at something deep inside me, something I've tried to bury for years.

I shift slightly, trying to ease the tension building in my body, but it only makes his smirk deepen. His head tilts slightly, studying me with an intensity that makes me feel completely exposed, even though the water is supposed to hide me.

"You're nervous," he says, his voice softer now, almost teasing, but there's an edge of sincerity beneath it. His fingers flex on the stone, his knuckles brushing against the edge of my shoulder in a way that sends a jolt through me.

I lift my chin, trying to reclaim some sense of control. "And you're too close."

His smirk doesn't falter, but his gaze softens slightly, the red in his eyes dimming just a fraction. "You've always been bad at lying, Raya," he says quietly, his voice dipping even lower, carrying an almost affectionate undertone.

The warmth in my chest spreads, and I hate the way he affects me so easily, the way he always has. But I can't deny the pull between us, the way his presence makes everything else fade away, even the lingering shadows of my fear.

"What do you want, Rhadis?" I ask, my voice steadier now, though my pulse betrays me, thundering in my ears.

His smirk fades entirely, replaced by something heavier, something real. "You," he says softly, his eyes searching mine, "it's always been you."

The words hang between us, wrapping around the tension like a thread, pulling it tighter. I want to say something, to ask him what he means, but the weight of his gaze keeps the words trapped in my throat. Instead, I stay still, letting the moment wash over me, feeling the heat of him, the quiet power in his voice, and the undeniable connection that has always lingered between us.

Rhadis's gaze doesn't waver as he leans in, the space between us shrinking until I can feel the faint heat of his breath against my lips. My heart pounds wildly in my chest, the lake and its warm waters forgotten as the world narrows down to him—his eyes, his presence, the way his closeness makes my entire body feel alive in ways I don't know how to describe.

But just as his lips brush mine, I place my hand on his chest, stopping him.

His eyes flicker with something I can't quite name—concern, confusion, or perhaps a flicker of frustration. "What is it?" he murmurs, his voice low and soft, like he's afraid of scaring me off.

"I'm not used to this," I admit, my voice barely above a whisper. "To… being close like this. To it feeling good."

His brows lift slightly, curiosity flickering across his face. "What do you mean?"

I hesitate, the words tangled in my throat. "I've been touched before," I say quietly. "But not like this. Never… for me."

His jaw tightens, his gaze sharpening with a dangerous edge. "Touched?" he echoes, his voice low and controlled, though I can feel the storm brewing beneath the surface.

"As a servant," I clarify, the words bitter on my tongue. "You know how lords can be. They take what they want, whether you want to give it or not."

His hand moves to cup my face, his thumb brushing lightly over my cheek. "No one will ever take from you again," he says, his tone laced with quiet fury. "Not while I'm here. Not while you're mine."

The possessiveness in his voice sends a shiver through me, but it's not fear that blooms in my chest—it's safety. The promise in his words feels like a shield, strong and unyielding.

"I've never been touched for me," I whisper, my voice trembling. "Not until you."

His eyes soften, the red ring around his pupils glowing faintly in the dim light. "Then let me show you," he murmurs, leaning closer. "Let me teach you what it means to be wanted. To be cared for."

Before I can respond, before I can even process the weight of his words, he leans in again, his movements slow and deliberate, giving me time to stop him.

But I don't.

I can't.

Something in me refuses to pull away.

His lips seal over mine, firm and warm, and everything in me seems to still and explode all at once. The kiss is soft at first, a gentle exploration that's almost at odds with the strength I've always seen in him. His hand rises to cup my face, his thumb brushing lightly against my cheek, and it's like he's trying to tell me something without words.

My fingers curl against his chest, grasping at the smooth planes of his skin as I feel myself melting into the kiss. It's overwhelming, this closeness, this intimacy, but it's not scary. It's Rhadis—his scent, his warmth, his steady presence—and for the first time in a long time, I feel safe and alive all at once.

The kiss deepens slightly, his lips moving against mine with a confidence that leaves no room for hesitation. He's guiding me, showing me, and I follow instinctively, letting myself get lost in the moment. It's everything and nothing like I expected, a strange mix of tenderness and possession, and I don't know if it's him or me or both, but I feel like I'm falling into something I'll never be able to climb out of.

When he finally pulls back, his forehead rests against mine, his breaths mingling with mine as the warm waters ripple gently around us. He doesn't say anything at first, just looks at me with those dark, intense eyes that seem to see straight through me.

"Now you're mine," he murmurs, his voice rough with emotion, the words a statement, not a question. And for the life of me, I can't bring myself to argue.

I blink up at him, my lips still tingling from his kiss, my heart racing as his words echo in my ears. *Now you're mine.* The weight of them lingers, heavy and undeniable, and I feel a surge of heat spreading through me—not just from his touch, but from the raw power behind what he's saying.

"What does that mean?" I ask softly, my voice trembling slightly but firm enough to carry. "To be yours?"

Rhadis's smirk returns, slow and deliberate, his red-ringed eyes locking onto mine with an intensity that makes the water feel hotter around me. His hand slides from my cheek to the side of my neck, his thumb brushing lightly over my pulse as if to remind me how thoroughly he has me in this moment.

"It means," he says, his voice low and steady, "you're mine to please. Mine to protect. Mine to do with as I wish."

The heat in my core flares at his words, an unfamiliar ache blooming in places I've never acknowledged before. But as powerful as his presence is, as consuming as the moment feels, something in me pushes back, refusing to be swept away entirely. I take a breath, willing my body to calm, to steady.

I press my hand against his chest, creating just enough space between us to meet his gaze fully. "No," I say, my voice stronger now. "I am my own. And only I will decide what you can or cannot do with me."

Rhadis freezes, his eyes narrowing slightly, not in anger but in surprise. It's as though he's weighing my words, testing them against whatever expectations he had. For a moment, the tension between us feels like it could snap, like the power dynamic is shifting in ways neither of us fully understands yet.

"But if I am to be yours," I continue, my voice steady despite the fluttering in my chest, "then you are mine. All the same. I won't be a submissive part of this... whatever this is between us." I gesture between us, my hand trembling slightly but my resolve holding firm. "If we are something, Rhadis, we are equals. You don't own me. Not entirely. I am my own person in this as well."

His smirk fades completely, replaced by something darker, something deeper. His fingers tighten just slightly on the side of my neck, not enough to hurt but enough to remind me of his strength, of the power he wields so effortlessly. For a moment, I wonder if I've pushed too far, if I've made a mistake.

But then, he tilts his head, a low chuckle escaping his lips. It's not mocking or cruel—it's full of something closer to admiration. "You always did have fire in you," he murmurs, his voice quieter now, though no less commanding. "Even when we were children. I suppose I shouldn't have expected anything less."

I hold his gaze, refusing to back down, and he seems to recognize it. His thumb brushes over my pulse again, softer this time, almost soothing. "Fine," he says, his tone shifting into something more thoughtful. "If you are mine, then yes, I am yours. All of me. My strength, my loyalty, my protection."

He leans in closer, his forehead almost touching mine, his voice dropping even lower. "But you should know something, Raya. I don't take this lightly. If you're mine—and I'm yours—it's forever. There's no halfway with me. No going back."

The scent of him lingers in the air, a mix of warmth and sandalwood, adding to the intensity of the moment. His words settle over me like a heavy cloak, a weight and a promise all at once. They stir something deep inside me, like a delicate tremor running through my veins. I search his face for any sign of deception, my fingertips tingling with anticipation. But all I see is truth, pure and unyielding.

"I wouldn't expect anything less," I say softly, my voice steady but laced with something raw, something vulnerable. As I speak, I feel a gentle warmth spreading on the top of my arm, accompanied by a tingling sensation. I look down, and there it is —a black band, a mate mark, acknowledging our bond. Showing me that the pull I have felt for him since we were children was real, destined by the fates long before I could have known. The touch of this mark on my skin sends a shiver down my spine. When I raise my gaze, I see the same mark etched deep and pitch black along his dark skin, a symbol of our connection in this life and all that follow.

For a moment, the world around us seems to hold its breath. The warm embrace of the water envelops us, its gentle ripples creating a soothing melody that fills the air. His presence overwhelms me, but not in an unwelcome way. It's like being cocooned in a sense of belonging, a feeling that I have found my place. Though there are still unanswered questions, one thing is certain: whatever this is between us, it's undeniably real. And this moment is just the beginning of our journey together.

Rhadis's eyes darken, the red rings around his pupils glowing faintly in the soft light of the cavern. He leans in again, his lips brushing against mine with a new intensity, not gentle this time but firm, commanding. The kiss deepens almost immediately, his tongue flicking past my lips, and a gasp escapes me. The sound seems to fuel him, his body pressing closer to mine until I can feel the heat and strength of his body against my skin.

There's nothing hesitant about this kiss—it's full of purpose, of dominance, and I can feel the weight of his intent in every movement. He's not just kissing me; he's claiming me, claiming the moment, showing me exactly who he is and what he's capable of. My hands press against his chest, a half-hearted attempt to create space, but the power in his presence pulls me in, overwhelming and consuming.

I try to push more into the kiss, to match his intensity, to show him that I'm not someone to simply be taken. My hands move from his chest to his shoulders, gripping tightly as I kiss him back, meeting his fervor with my own. But just as I think I'm gaining ground, he tilts my head back with a firm grip on my hair, his fingers weaving through the strands with practiced ease.

The move is effortless, confident, and it forces me to bare my throat to him, leaving me exposed in a way that sends a shiver through my entire body. I feel the tension in my core grow, a heat spreading that I can't control, even as I try to resist the pull of his dominance. He takes full control of the kiss, his lips and tongue moving against mine with a precision that leaves no room for doubt—he is in charge.

I lose myself in him, the strength of his grip, the way his body presses me against the stone behind me, grounding me and overwhelming me all at once. My thoughts scatter, every logical piece of myself slipping away as the kiss deepens further. It's not just physical—it's emotional, charged with years of unspoken tension and the now permanent connection that has always existed between us.

When he finally pulls back, just enough for us to breathe, his forehead rests against mine, his breathing heavy. My chest rises and falls as I try to catch my breath, my fingers still in his hair, my lips tingling from the force of his kiss. He doesn't say anything, but his gaze locks onto mine, his eyes searching my face as though he's waiting for me to say something, to question the bond—or to pull him closer.

Rhadis's breathing slows, his forehead still resting against mine. The warmth of his skin radiates into me, his presence enveloping me like a shadow, dark but comforting. His hand loosens slightly in my hair, brushing gently along the strands before coming to rest on my cheek. His eyes, still glowing faintly with that haunting red ring, soften as he looks at me.

"I've always known," he murmurs, his voice low and raw with something deeper than desire—something more vulnerable. "That we were mates."

The words hit me like a lightning strike, my breath catching in my throat. I pull back slightly to study his face, searching for any hint of uncertainty, but all I see is the quiet resolve of a truth he's carried for a long time.

"You've known?" I ask, my voice trembling, though I'm not sure if it's from surprise or the lingering effects of his kiss.

He nods, his thumb brushing over my cheek in a soothing motion. "I've known since we were young, Raya. But I couldn't...

I wouldn't accept the bond until you did. Until you were ready. I've watched over you, protecting you as I could until I thought the time was right. Until now."

His words sink into me slowly, the weight of them filling the space between us. He's been waiting—watching, protecting, always staying close, even when I didn't realize it. The depth of his patience, of his restraint, is staggering.

I feel a faint warmth on my arm and glance down, still startled to see the black mark encircling my bicep, now pulsing faintly, as if responding to his closeness. The band, dark and bold against my pale skin, seems alive now, its rhythm matching the quiet thrum of my heart. I lift my arm slightly, turning it to watch the mark move like it is full of living shadows, as though it's drawing strength from him and his powers.

I meet his gaze again, and this time, a small smile tugs at my lips despite the storm of emotions inside me. "You've waited all this time?" I ask softly, my voice barely above a whisper.

"For you?" he replies, his lips curving into a faint smile of his own. "I would have waited forever."

The mark pulses again, a steady rhythm that feels like it's binding us together, and I can't help but feel a flicker of something I haven't let myself feel in a long time—hope. It's as if the mark recognizes what I've been too afraid to admit: that this bond, this connection between us, is real, undeniable, and something I don't want to fight anymore.

My smile grows, soft but genuine, and I lift my hand to trace the edge of his jaw, feeling the slight roughness of his skin beneath my fingertips. “I think I’ve always known too,” I admit quietly, the words falling from my lips before I can stop them.

His expression shifts, the smirk fading into something deeper, something almost reverent. He leans in, pressing a kiss to my forehead, and I close my eyes, letting the moment wash over me. The weight of the years, the distance, the uncertainty—all of it seems to melt away, leaving only us.

“You’re mine,” he whispers against my skin, the words no longer a claim, but a vow.

“And you’re mine,” I reply, my voice steady and certain, the truth of it sinking into my very core.

The mark pulses again, a quiet reminder of the bond we’ve both finally accepted, and for the first time, I feel like I’ve found something I didn’t even know I was missing.

CHAPTER FOUR

The air is crisp and cool as we step out of the cave, the night wrapping around us like a velvet cloak. The stars are scattered across the sky, their faint light glimmering against the dark peaks of the mountains. Rhadis's hand rests lightly on my hip as we walk, his touch grounding, steady, yet electric. The warmth of his skin sends little shocks through me, a reminder of the hours we spent in the water together, the way we seemed to forget the world beyond the cave.

He leans close, his voice low and soft. "Close your eyes."

I hesitate for only a moment before obeying. The familiar sensation of his magic stirs around me, dark and whispering, but never causing any fear or nerves. It envelops me like a shadow, warm and all-encompassing, and when it fades, the crisp night air is replaced by the scent of cedarwood and stone.

I open my eyes to see the towering silhouette of Rhadis's home, its dark spires cutting into the night sky. The heavy doors are just ahead of us, their iron details gleaming faintly in the moonlight.

"No gifts or powers can send people inside these walls," Rhadis says, his voice quieter now, almost contemplative. "Not even mine. This is the one place that remains untouched."

The weight of his words lingers in the air as he opens the door and guides me inside. The warmth of the entryway surrounds us instantly, the scent of faint incense mixed with the cool stone floors. We walk in silence, our footsteps echoing faintly as we ascend the grand staircase. His hand never leaves my hip, a steady presence as he leads me upward.

As we pass a large wooden door on the second floor, faint sounds filter through the thick wood—soft moans followed by a deep male groan. My eyes widen, my face heating instantly as I realize what I'm hearing. Rhadis notices immediately, a smirk curling at the corner of his mouth.

"Ryat and Emory," he murmurs, amusement lacing his tone as my steps quicken, eager to put some distance between us and the sounds. My cheeks burn, but I don't look back, even as I hear Rhadis's low laugh behind me.

He catches up easily, his hand brushing against my lower back as he guides me down the hall. "Mated pairs are… spirited," he teases, his voice warm with humor.

I glare at him over my shoulder. "Not another word," I warn, though the embarrassment in my voice weakens the threat.

When we reach his room, the tension fades as he pushes the door open, revealing the familiar space. The faint scent of lavender and wood lingers in the air, and the flickering light of lanterns casting long shadows across the walls. Rhadis steps inside, turning to face me.

"Would you like a bath before bed?" he asks, his voice softer now, void of teasing. There's something almost tender in the way he looks at me, as though he knows the day has been long and overwhelming.

I nod. "Yes, I'd like that."

He gestures toward the armoire. "There should be nightgowns in there for you. The servants stocked it earlier. Take your time and grab one if you would like to sleep clothed." He moves toward the bathing chamber, his movements fluid and purposeful, leaving me to explore.

I open the armoire, finding a neatly arranged selection of nightgowns and dresses in soft, luxurious fabrics. I choose a pale cream gown, simple but elegant, the material smooth against my fingertips. As I hold it, my curiosity pulls me toward the bathing chamber, and I step through the doorway.

The room is warm and inviting, just as it had been for me earlier today. The large black marble tub dominates the space, its surface shimmering with steaming water that flows from the carved fountain at the end. The scent of lavender and eucalyptus fills the air, mingling with the faint sweetness of the bubbles frothing across the water's surface. Candles line the counter next to the tub, their golden light dancing softly against the light sage walls.

Rhadis stands by the edge of the tub, his sleeves rolled up as he adjusts something near the fountain. He glances over his shoulder when he hears me enter, his gaze softening when it meets mine.

"I added some oils," he says, gesturing toward the tub. "Relaxing ones. The water's just the right temperature now."

I look at the space, at the effort he's gone through to make it feel like more than just a bath, and a quiet warmth fills my chest. He steps back, nodding toward the tub.

"Enjoy your bath," he says simply, his tone gentle as he heads toward the door. "I'll be on the cot if you need anything."

Before I can thank him, he's gone, leaving me alone in the serene glow of the bathing chamber. I step closer to the tub, running my fingers over the smooth edge of the marble as the steam rises around me. The water looks almost too inviting to resist, and as I set my nightgown aside and remove my corset and dress to step in, the warmth envelopes me completely, easing away the tension of the day.

For the first time in what feels like weeks, I let myself sink into the water and just breathe.

The water is perfectly warm as I soak in the tub, letting the heat seep into my muscles and chase away the tension of the day. The soft scent of lavender and eucalyptus fills the air, calming me as I let my head rest against the smooth edge of the tub. My mind drifts, swirling with the memories of the last few hours, the weight of everything still pressing lightly against me.

I glance at the counter beside the tub and notice a straight razor resting neatly on a small dish. It catches my attention, and I realize I hadn't thought to ask for one earlier. The thought of slipping into the cot feeling refreshed, without the slight prickle of my unshaved legs, is tempting. With a sigh, I decide to take advantage of it.

Carefully, I lather my legs with the soap left beside the razor, running the blade lightly over my skin. The process feels strangely soothing, the repetitive motion grounding me as I take my time. Once I've finished my legs, I move to the more intimate parts of myself, the warmth of the water and the lavender-scented bubbles making the task surprisingly relaxing.

When I'm done, I reach for the shampoo and conditioner left out for me. The bottles are simple but elegant, the scent of the products as luxurious as the rest of the bath. I work the shampoo into my hair, the lather rich and silky, before rinsing it away and following with the conditioner. The strands feel soft and clean beneath my fingers, and for a moment, I lose myself in the simple pleasure of the routine.

Finally, I step out of the tub, the cool air of the room brushing against my damp skin. I grab one of the fluffy towels folded neatly on the counter and wrap it around myself, the fabric thick and warm as I dry off. Once I'm dry, I pull on the cream nightgown I'd chosen earlier, the smooth fabric sliding over my skin like a whisper. It's comfortable, modest but elegant, and I find myself smoothing it over my hips as I take one last glance at the bathing chamber before stepping out.

When I enter the room, the first thing I notice is Rhadis. He's lying on the cot, the furs bunched lazily around his hips, his chest bare and catching the faint flicker of candlelight. The sight sends a flutter through my chest, though I tell myself it's nothing. He's reclined back with a book in his hands, his expression focused, the faint lines of concentration softening his otherwise sharp features.

He glances up as I approach, his dark eyes meeting mine. "Feeling better?" he asks, his voice low and casual.

I nod, crossing the room and slipping into the cot beside him. The furs are warm against my skin, and I settle a few inches away, unsure of what he might expect from me tonight. He doesn't move closer, though, simply watching me for a moment before returning to his book.

After a moment of silence, he tilts his head slightly. "Do you want to read?" he asks, holding up the book.

I shake my head, resting my hand lightly over my stomach. "No, I think I have a bit of an ache in my eyes," I admit, my voice soft.

He pauses, studying me briefly, and then his lips curve into a faint smile. "Would you like me to read to you?"

The offer surprises me, but I nod. "Yes," I say, my voice barely above a whisper.

Rhadis shifts slightly, his tone softening as he begins to read. His voice is low and smooth, each word rolling off his tongue with an ease that's almost hypnotic. The story is fictional, but the vivid descriptions and the emotion in his voice draw me in. It's about a man carrying a newborn child through a desert, the harshness of the journey contrasting with the tender way he speaks to the baby.

I close my eyes as I listen, letting the cadence of Rhadis's voice wash over me. But then, he stops suddenly. The abrupt silence pulls me out of my half-relaxed state, and I glance up at him, confused.

"Why did you stop?" I ask softly, my brow furrowing.

Rhadis doesn't answer immediately. His gaze fixed on the book, his expression soft. After a moment, he looks at me, his dark eyes filled with something I can't quite place.

"You're too far away" he begins, his voice quieter now, "I am missing your touch."

There's a softness in his tone, a vulnerability I've never heard from him before. It makes my chest tighten, and I find myself reaching out, my hand brushing against his wrist.

"I do not need to be so far," I say lightly. "Where would you like me to be?"

He smiles, closing the book with deliberate care and setting it aside. The moment hangs between us, thick with unspoken words, and as I lie back against the furs, I wonder just how much more there is to Rhadis that I've yet to understand.

He shifts beside me, his arm sliding around my shoulders as he pulls me closer. The movement is natural, unspoken, and before I can even think to question it, my head is resting on his bare chest. His skin is warm beneath my cheek, his steady heartbeat a soothing rhythm that echoes in my ears. I don't resist. The comfort of his presence, his calm strength, feels like a balm to my restless thoughts.

His other hand finds its way to my hair, his fingers weaving through the damp strands with a gentleness that takes me by surprise. The slow, repetitive motion is hypnotic, his touch light but grounding, like he's silently reassuring me that I'm safe here, with him.

"This is exactly what I've needed," he murmurs, his voice soft, almost tender, as though he's speaking more to the air than to me.

I let out a breath I hadn't realized I was holding, my body sinking further into the warmth of his embrace. The faint scent of him fills my senses, and I close my eyes, letting it calm me. The tension I didn't even know I was carrying begins to melt away.

After a moment, I hear the soft rustle of paper as he picks up the book again. His voice starts quietly, the same low, measured tone that feels like it's meant just for me. He reads without pause, his words flowing seamlessly, painting vivid pictures of desert skies and golden sands, of struggle and perseverance, of love and hope.

The story wraps around me, but it's his voice that holds me, steady and sure, like an anchor in a storm. The deep resonance of it seeps into my skin, blending with the warmth of his hand in my hair, the steady rise and fall of his chest beneath me.

My eyelids grow heavier with each word, the soft cadence of his voice pulling me toward sleep. I fight it at first, not wanting to lose the moment, but the exhaustion of the day catches up with me. The last thing I feel before slipping into the quiet embrace of dreams is the steady stroke of his fingers through my hair and the soft rumble of his voice—a warmth I didn't know I needed, but one I can't imagine being without now.

CHAPTER FIVE

I wake slowly, the soft light of dawn filtering into the room, and the first thing I notice is the heat. A strong, solid warmth presses against my back, and for a moment, I'm too groggy to understand why. My body feels heavy, wrapped in a cocoon of soft furs and the steady, rhythmic sound of someone breathing behind me.

Then I shift slightly, and something firm presses against my backside.

A low groan rumbles behind me, deep and rich, and I freeze. The memory of where I am and who I'm with crashes over me all at once.

"Rhadis," I murmur, my voice hoarse from sleep.

"Stay still," he murmurs, his voice rough and quiet, a hint of amusement threading through it. "Let me enjoy holding you like this a bit longer."

I feel my cheeks burn, the heat traveling down my neck. "I can feel you," I whisper, the words escaping before I can stop them.

My face flushes even more when I realize how ridiculous I sound, but I can't bring myself to say anything else.

Rhadis chuckles softly, the sound low and unbothered, vibrating through his chest against my back. "Good," he says, and I can practically hear the smirk in his voice.

I push back slightly, intending to shift away, but the movement only presses me closer to him, and I hear him groan again. "You're not helping," he mutters, his tone somewhere between frustration and amusement.

I feel like my face might catch fire. "I mean, I can feel you," I say again, a little louder this time, my voice almost cracking. "Your... manhood."

This time, his laugh is louder, and I feel it reverberate against me. "That's normal," he says casually, as though this is the most natural conversation in the world. "For a male waking up with a gorgeous female in his cot. Especially when she is his mate."

My breath catches, and I'm grateful he can't see my face right now because I know it must be glowing. "It's hard as steel. Does it... hurt?" I ask hesitantly, the question tumbling out before I can think it through. I've never thought about how it feels for a male to be so hard, never cared until now.

His laugh deepens, rich and warm, and I feel him shift slightly behind me, his arm tightening around my waist. "Not painful, no," he says, his tone still carrying that teasing edge. "Just... uncomfortable. I'm aroused."

The casual way he says it only makes me blush harder, and I

press my hands against the furs, trying to find something solid to hold onto as the weight of his words sinks in. I don't know how to respond, my mind torn between embarrassment and the strange fluttering sensation his proximity is stirring in me.

"You're aroused?" I ask quietly, almost to myself.

His voice softens slightly, though the teasing doesn't disappear entirely. "Raya," he says, his tone almost exasperated. "I'm a man. You're my beautiful mate. We're sharing a cot, and I've spent the night holding you. What do you think?"

I bite my lip, the warmth spreading through me both mortifying and strangely comforting. There's no malice in his words, no threat—just honesty, simple and straightforward, like everything else about him.

I shift again, this time to sit up, and he lets me go, though his hand lingers on my hip for a moment before falling away. I don't dare look at him, afraid of what I might see, but his presence is still there, steady and close, and I can feel his eyes on me as I try to gather my scattered thoughts.

"You're impossible," I mutter, though there's no bite in my voice, only a quiet exasperation.

"And yet, here you are," he replies smoothly, his voice laced with amusement.

I glance back at him finally, catching the faint smirk on his lips and the warmth in his eyes, and for a moment, I forget why I was embarrassed in the first place. There's something in his expression—something real, unguarded—that makes it impossible to stay angry.

I sit back against the pillows, clutching the soft furs draped over my lap as I gather the courage to speak. My gaze drifts to Rhadis, his broad chest illuminated by the faint light filtering through the room. His expression is calm, but his eyes are locked on me with an intensity that makes my heart race. It's as though he's already waiting for me to speak, sensing the unease building inside me.

"Does it... bother you?" I ask hesitantly, my voice quieter than I intended. "That I don't have experience? That everything I know is about how to please a man, but nothing about... myself?"

His lips curve into a faint smile, one that's warm and reassuring rather than mocking. "No," he says simply, his voice steady and honest. "If anything, I'm glad."

I blink, surprised. "Why?"

He leans forward slightly, resting his forearms on his knees as his gaze remains steady. "Because it means I get to be the one to change that," he murmurs. "To teach you how intimacy can feel when it's about you. To show you what you've never been allowed to experience."

Heat rushes to my cheeks, and I glance away, suddenly feeling exposed. The weight of his words, the sincerity in his voice—it's overwhelming. I tug at the edge of the furs, twisting the fabric in my hands as I try to steady myself.

"There are... ways to be close," I venture hesitantly, stumbling over the words. "Without... everything, right?"

His expression softens further, and he reaches out to gently brush a strand of hair from my face. The touch is light, deliberate, and sends a shiver down my spine. “There are many ways to build connection,” he says softly. “To explore intimacy without crossing boundaries you’re not ready for. This is about us—what you want, not what anyone else has made you think it has to be.”

His words settle over me like a balm, soothing the nervous energy coursing through me. I nod slowly, my fingers tightening on the furs as I force myself to ask the question I’ve been holding back. “Will you… show me?”

For a moment, his smirk returns, though it’s tempered by something tender. “If that’s what you want,” he murmurs, his voice low and intimate. “Then yes, I would love to.”

I nod again, unable to find the words to answer aloud. The nervous fluttering in my chest mingles with anticipation as he shifts closer, his hands firm but gentle as he pulls me toward him. He cradles my face in his hands, tilting my head up to meet his lips in a kiss that quickly deepens. It’s unhurried, deliberate, and full of a warmth I hadn’t known I craved.

His hands move slowly, one trailing down to rest on my shoulder while the other brushes the edge of my nightgown. His fingers pause there, giving me a chance to stop him, but when I don’t, he lifts the fabric over my head. The cool air brushes against my skin, but it’s his gaze that truly makes me feel exposed.

“You’re stunning,” he murmurs, his eyes roving over me as though he’s committing every detail to memory. “So beautiful.”

The sincerity in his voice steals my breath, and I try to focus on the feeling of his hands as they begin to explore. His fingers trace the line of my collarbone, down to my chest, before cupping my breast. The first touch is soft, almost reverent, but when his thumb brushes over my nipple, a jolt of sensation shoots through me.

I gasp, my hands gripping his arms for support as heat flares in my core. His gaze flicks up to mine, sharp and assessing, as though he's gauging every reaction, every flicker of emotion on my face.

"This is for you, Raya," he says softly, his tone laced with something darker. "No one else."

His hands begin to move with more purpose, alternating between gentle caresses and firmer squeezes. I can feel my body responding to his touch in ways I don't fully understand, the ache in my core building with every brush of his thumb over my sensitive skin. My breath quickens, my chest rising and falling beneath his hands, and I bite my lip to keep from making a sound.

But when he pinches my nipple, the sharp mix of pleasure and pain makes me moan aloud. The sound startles me as much as it seems to delight him, his lips quirking into a faint smirk as his hands move with newfound confidence. My hips shift slightly, pressing into nothing, chasing a relief I didn't even realize I needed. The ache in my core deepens, a steady, pulsing warmth that builds with every movement of his hands.

"You like that," he murmurs, his voice low and teasing. "Good.

Let yourself feel it."

I try to focus, to hold on to some semblance of control, but the heat spreading through me is all-consuming. His hands trail lower, brushing over the curve of my stomach before resting between my thighs. My breath catches, my entire body tensing as his fingers explore gently, teasingly.

"You're so beautiful like this," he says, his voice rough with emotion. His fingers trace the curve of my breast, his gaze dipping to watch the way my chest rises and falls with each unsteady breath. "I could spend hours learning every part of you."

When he strokes my sex for the first time, a wave of sensation crashes over me, leaving me trembling in his arms. "Rhadis," I gasp, my voice shaky and raw.

"Look at me," he says, his voice commanding but gentle. "I want to see you."

I force my eyes open, meeting his gaze, and the red ring around his pupils glows faintly, a reflection of the intensity building between us. His fingers stroke me again, firmer this time, and the pleasure building inside me shatters. My body shakes uncontrollably as I cry out, waves of sensation crashing over me in a way I never thought possible. I cry out, the sound raw and desperate, as my head falls against his chest. But even in the haze of pleasure, his words pull me back.

"Look at me, Raya," he says again, his voice deeper now, filled with a dark kind of urgency.

I force my head to tilt back, my body still trembling, and meet his gaze once more. The glowing red rings around his pupils seem almost alive, swirling with an otherworldly light that captivates and consumes me. There's power in his eyes, a raw, primal force that makes my pulse race even faster, but there's something else there too—something protective, something that feels like it's just for me.

"That's it," he murmurs, his voice softer now, soothing as his fingers continue their slow, deliberate strokes. "Let it happen. Don't hold back."

I don't have the strength to respond, my body still shaking as wave after wave of pleasure courses through me. The glowing red in his eyes intensifies, pulling me in deeper, and all I can do is cling to the moment, to him, as everything else fades away.

When it's over, he holds me against his chest, his touch soothing as he strokes my back. I feel vulnerable, exposed—but for the first time, I also feel cherished, seen. I rest my head against his shoulder, letting the steady rhythm of his breathing calm me as I whisper, "I didn't know it could feel like this."

His arms tighten around me, his lips pressing softly against my temple. "With me, it always will."

His fingers trace idle patterns along my skin, warm and soothing. "How do you feel?" he asks, his voice low and intimate, laced with curiosity and care. "Was there anything you liked more? Or something you'd want to try again?"

I tilt my head up, catching the faint glimmer of mischief in his glowing eyes. His red-ringed gaze holds mine, searching for something genuine, something real in my response. I can't help the soft laugh that escapes me, my body still buzzing faintly.

"How do I feel?" I repeat, my voice breathless. "I feel... incredible. Like nothing I've ever imagined." I pause, my cheeks warming as I lower my gaze to his collarbone. "But I don't think I can do anything else right now. My body feels like jelly."

His laugh rumbles through his chest, deep and rich, vibrating against my cheek where it rests. "Jelly?" he repeats, his tone laced with amusement. "I'm glad I was able to 'jellify' you so early in the morning."

I can't help but laugh again, the sound light and free, though my limbs still feel like they might give out if I tried to move. "That's not a real word, you know."

"It is now," he says, a smug grin tugging at his lips. "A very important word, actually. A milestone, if you will."

I roll my eyes, though the smile on my face betrays me. "You're impossible."

"So you've said," he teases, brushing a stray strand of hair from my face. His hand lingers for a moment, his touch soft, before it drifts back to my arm. "I'm glad you enjoyed yourself," he adds, his tone softening, becoming more genuine. "It's important to me that you do."

His words make my chest tighten, a warmth blooming there that has nothing to do with what just happened. I feel safe here, in his arms, and it's a feeling I didn't realize I was missing until now.

"I did," I admit quietly, my fingers curling lightly against his chest. "More than I thought I would."

"Good," he murmurs, pressing a soft kiss to the top of my head. "We'll take our time, Raya. There's no rush, no pressure. Only what you want."

The sincerity in his voice makes my heart ache in the best way. I nod against him, letting his words settle over me like a fur, warm and reassuring. For now, it's enough just to be here, held against him, with nothing but the steady rhythm of his heartbeat and the quiet promise of more to come.

The warmth of Rhadis' chest fades reluctantly as he shifts, moving to sit up. I sigh softly, feeling the absence of his touch even as I gather myself to follow him. The morning light filtering through the curtains paints the room in golden hues, and I watch as Rhadis pulls on a loose black shirt, the fabric clinging to his strong frame in a way that makes my cheeks warm.

He glances at me with that ever-present smirk, extending a hand to help me up. "Come on," he says, his voice low and teasing. "We've got a day to start."

I let him pull me to my feet, and when I reach for a light green dress in the armoire, he takes it from me. "Let me," he says softly, his voice gentler now. I nod, letting him guide the dress over my head and down my body. His fingers linger at the fabric's edges, smoothing it over my shoulders and waist before he kneels to adjust the hem and slide on my boots.

It's an intimacy I didn't expect, quiet and unspoken, and it stirs something deep within me—something that feels even stronger than the glowing mark encircling my arm.

When we're ready, Rhadis leads me downstairs, his hand resting lightly on the small of my back. The scent of warm bread and faint spices drifts through the halls as we enter the dining room. Just like yesterday, he pulls out my chair and waits for me to settle before taking the seat beside me. It's a simple gesture, but it speaks volumes.

I barely have a moment to settle before a loud gasp fills the room. I turn just in time to see Emory hurrying toward me, her silver hair bouncing around her shoulders, her expression alight with curiosity and excitement.

"Raya!" she exclaims, her eyes fixed on my arm. "When did that happen?"

It takes me a moment to understand what she means, and when I do, my cheeks flush. I glance at the mark—still dark and pulsing faintly, a constant reminder of everything that happened yesterday. My mind flashes back to the cave, to the way Rhadis's hands felt on me, his kiss, his words... My face grows even hotter.

"Yesterday afternoon," I admit quietly, unable to meet her eyes as the memory surges through me.

Emory's face lights up, and she claps her hands together. "I'm so happy for you!" she says, her joy genuine and infectious.

I glance at Rhadis, who leans back in his chair with a faint smirk, clearly amused by my reaction. Before I can say anything, Ryat speaks up from across the table, his deep voice calm and steady.

"It's a special bond," he says, his gaze shifting between Rhadis and me. "Appreciate the newness of it. The first days are unlike anything else." He pauses, his expression softening. "And when you're ready, you'll have your ceremony."

My breath catches at the mention of a ceremony. I hadn't even thought that far ahead. The weight of the bond, of what it means, is still sinking in. I glance at Rhadis again, and his smirk softens into something quieter, something just for me.

"We will," he says, his voice steady but firm, a promise in the words. "When the time is right."

Emory beams, reaching out to squeeze my hand. "It's going to be beautiful, Raya," she says, her voice full of warmth. "I know it will be."

Her words stir a mix of emotions in me—anticipation, nervousness, and something else I can't quite name. But as I glance at Rhadis, his dark eyes steady and sure, I feel a flicker of certainty. Whatever the future holds, I know I won't be facing it alone.

The conversation at the table shifts to lighter topics, with Emory and Ryat talking about preparations for their upcoming child. I'm half-listening, still replaying Emory's words about the ceremony and what it might mean for Rhadis and me, when a servant enters the room. He moves quietly, carrying a small rolled parchment in his hands.

"My lord," the servant says, inclining his head as he hands the message to Rhadis.

Rhadis accepts it with a nod, his posture still relaxed as he unfurls the parchment. But as his eyes skim over the words, his entire body tenses. The playful smirk that had graced his lips moments ago vanishes, replaced by a sharp, unreadable expression.

I sit up straighter, a strange unease prickling at the back of my neck. "What is it?" I ask softly, but he doesn't respond immediately. His eyes are locked on the parchment, the muscles in his jaw tightening.

Unable to wait, I lean over, my heart racing as I glance at the letter. The words are clear and concise, but they carry a weight that sinks into my chest as I read them.

Lord Rhadis,

A group of gifted have escaped from the southern prison. They have made their way to the eastern borders and are believed to be gathering strength. Containment efforts have failed. Immediate action is required.

SR Alken

I look up at him, searching his face. "The prisoners escaped?" I whisper, my voice tinged with disbelief. "How could that happen?"

Rhadis sets the parchment down on the table with a measured calm that feels anything but reassuring. His dark eyes flick to the group gathered around us, and when he speaks, his tone is authoritative, sharp.

“There’s been an issue at the prisons,” he announces, his voice cutting through the hum of conversation. “It will require my attention for a while.”

The room falls silent as everyone absorbs his words. Emory glances at me, worry etched across her face, while Ryat leans back in his chair, his brows furrowing.

Rhadis pushes his chair back, standing slowly. “Make yourselves at home. You’re safe here,” he continues, addressing the table. “I’ll return when I can.”

As he moves to leave, I rise to my feet, my hand reaching for his arm. “Wait,” I say, my voice firm but laced with concern. “You’re going alone? Let me come with you.”

His gaze softens slightly as he looks at me, but his answer is immediate. “No.”

“No?” I repeat, my voice rising slightly. “Rhadis, you don’t even know what you’re walking into. You will be outnumbered—”

“I said no, Raya,” he interrupts, his voice dropping, quieter but no less commanding. He steps closer, lowering his voice further so only I can hear. “You can’t come with me. It’s not up for debate.”

I glare at him, anger and worry mixing in my chest. “Why not? You don’t trust me? Or do you think I’ll just slow you down?”

His lips press into a thin line, and for a moment, he seems to weigh his words carefully. "It's not about trust," he says finally, his tone softening. "It's about keeping you safe. You're my mate now, and your safety comes first. Always."

The sincerity in his voice makes my resolve waver, but only slightly. "I can take care of myself," I insist, though my voice falters.

"I know," he says, his hand brushing lightly against my cheek. "But not this time."

Before I can argue further, the air around him shifts, charged with the unmistakable energy of his magic. The shadows seem to gather around him, and his familiar scent—dark and earthy, tinged with a faint sweetness—fills the air.

"Rhadis, wait—"

But it's too late. In the blink of an eye, he's gone, leaving only the faint trace of his magic lingering in the room. I stand there, frozen, my chest tight with frustration and worry.

The silence in the room feels oppressive, and when I finally turn back to the table, all eyes are on me. Emory rises, moving to my side, her hand resting lightly on my arm.

"Are you okay?" she asks softly, her silver eyes full of concern.

I nod, though the tightness in my chest doesn't ease.

"He'll be fine," I say, more to reassure myself than anyone else.

But even as I speak the words, the unease in my heart refuses to fade.

CHAPTER SIX

The water in the bath is warm, its soft lavender scent filling the room, but the tension in my chest refuses to ease. I sink deeper into the tub, letting my head rest against the smooth edge as I stare at the flickering candlelight. The room feels too quiet, the stillness amplifying the restless worry that churns in my stomach.

I've been here for what feels like hours, trying to stay awake, waiting for the sound of his return. But my body betrays me, exhaustion pulling at the edges of my consciousness. I drift in and out, the warmth of the water lulling me closer to sleep even as I fight it.

The faint sound of fabric rustling pulls me from the haze. My eyes flutter open, and it takes a moment for the room to come into focus. When it does, my breath catches.

Rhadis stands near the doorway, his back to me as he removes his shirt, the muscles in his shoulders shifting with the movement. The fabric is dark and stiff, and as he pulls it away, I see the unmistakable stains of blood smeared across it. My stomach drops, and I sit up quickly, the water sloshing gently around me.

“Are you injured?” I ask, my voice sharper than I intended. My heart races as my eyes search his bare back for wounds, but the flickering candlelight makes it hard to see clearly.

He pauses, glancing over his shoulder at me. His expression is calm, his dark eyes steady as he shakes his head. “The blood isn’t mine,” he says simply, his voice low but firm. “I wasn’t harmed.”

The relief that washes over me is immediate, but it’s quickly replaced by the stark reminder of what he’s been dealing with. “Whose blood is it?” I ask softly, though I’m not sure I want to know.

He doesn’t answer, at least not directly. Instead, he finishes untying and removing his pants, his movements slow and deliberate. The fabric falls to the floor with a soft rustle, joining his bloodied shirt. I can’t help but notice the tension in his body, the faint lines of exhaustion etched into his face as he steps toward the tub.

“Move forward,” he says gently, his tone leaving no room for argument.

I do as he asks, sliding forward to give him space. The water ripples as he climbs in behind me, his presence filling the small space as the warmth of his skin presses against my back. I feel his strong hands on my hips, guiding me until I’m resting against his chest, his arms wrapping loosely around my middle.

The faint pink tint of the water catches my eye, and I realize the blood still clinging to his skin is mixing with the bath water. "You should have rinsed before getting in," I murmur, my voice softer now, tinged with concern.

"I wanted to be near you," he replies, his voice low and raw. His fingers brush lightly along my arm, tracing the mark encircling my bicep. "I needed to feel you on my skin."

His words make my chest tighten, a quiet ache settling there. I lean back against him, my head resting on his shoulder as I let out a soft sigh. "Was it bad?" I ask hesitantly, my voice barely above a whisper.

He doesn't answer right away, his hand continuing its slow, soothing motions on my arm. "It's handled," he says eventually, his tone steady but distant. "That's all that matters."

I want to press him, to ask what he had to do, what he had to see, but the exhaustion in his voice keeps me quiet. Instead, I turn in the water, my hands brushing against Rhadis's chest as I shift to face him. The ripples from my movement lap softly against the edges of the tub, the warm water carrying the faint scent of lavender still. My gaze flicks up to meet his, and the faint glow of red around his pupils pulls at something deep inside me. His eyes are steady, watching me with an intensity that makes my stomach twist, but I try to focus on the task at hand.

I grab the cloth and soap resting on the edge of the tub, dipping them into the water. The warmth seeps into my fingers as I work the soap into a lather. Without speaking, I press the cloth to his chest, my hands moving slowly, deliberately. The dried blood that streaks his skin mixes with the water, swirling away in faint tendrils of pink. The sight unsettles me, but I push the feeling down, focusing instead on him—on the way his chest rises and falls under my touch, his muscles taut beneath my fingers.

I can feel the tension in him, the weight of whatever happened before he returned to me. His body is strong, unyielding, but I know it's been through so much. The scars that mark his skin tell a story I only know pieces of, and I wonder how many more battles he fought since we were children. How much of his strength has been forged through pain?

"Does this hurt?" I ask softly, my voice barely louder than a whisper as I rub the cloth over a particularly tight knot in his shoulder.

"No," he murmurs, his deep voice rumbling through me. "It feels good."

His words send a flicker of warmth through my chest, and I press a little harder, kneading the tension from his muscles. My hands are steady as I work, moving from his shoulders to his arms, washing away the remnants of the day while trying to give him some relief from whatever burdens he's carrying.

But as I continue, I become more aware of the quiet intimacy of the moment. The way his skin feels beneath my fingers, the heat of the water surrounding us, the way his eyes never leave my face. My heart beats faster as I trail the cloth lower, across the planes of his stomach, the soap-slicked water leaving his skin smooth and clean.

I reach his hips and pause, my hands hovering uncertainly over his skin. The water laps gently around us, the only sound in the room aside from the soft rasp of my breath. My gaze flickers upward, meeting his steady, expectant eyes. There's no impatience in his expression, no demand—just quiet patience, like he's waiting for me to make the first move.

"Can I…?" My voice falters, barely audible. The words hang between us, heavy and charged. My cheeks flush hot, and I drop my gaze, unable to meet his eyes. "Can I touch you?"

He doesn't answer immediately, but when he does, his voice is low and rough, almost reverent. "Yes."

The simple word sends a ripple of nerves and anticipation through me. My hands tremble slightly as I lower them into the water, the soap slipping between my fingers as I reach for him. When my fingers brush against him, I freeze. He's warm and firm beneath my touch, his body reacting instantly. The sound he makes—a low, guttural groan—sends a shiver racing down my spine, my own body responding to the raw power in that sound.

I move cautiously, unsure of what I'm doing but determined to try. I've never been forced to touch a male like this and I am so grateful that this will be my first experience, that I am sharing this first with my mate.

My fingers explore with deliberate slowness, the slickness of the soap making each movement feel smoother. The water ripples softly around us, a gentle backdrop to the quiet tension filling the air. Rhadis tilts his head back slightly, his dark hair brushing the edge of the tub, and the groan that escapes his lips makes my stomach flip.

My movements are tentative, each stroke an experiment, each reaction from him a reassurance. The tension in his body builds beneath my hands, his muscles taut and unyielding. It feels strange, foreign, but there's a growing confidence in the way he responds to me, in the way his breathing deepens and his grip on the edge of the tub tightens.

"Raya," he murmurs, my name leaving his lips like a quiet prayer. His voice is deeper now, rougher, and the sound tugs at something deep inside me.

I glance up to gauge his reaction, and the sight before me steals my breath. His head is tilted back, his jaw tight, and his eyes —when they open—are glowing faintly, the red ring around his pupils brighter now, more vivid. He looks utterly undone, his usual composure shattered, and the realization that I caused this sends a strange thrill coursing through me.

I continue, my strokes growing more confident, more deliberate. The water sloshes gently around us, mixing with the low, guttural sounds escaping him. My own nerves begin to fade, replaced by something else—a quiet sense of control, of power. The knowledge that I can affect him like this is intoxicating.

His breathing grows heavier, his body tensing beneath my hands, and I feel the shift in him, the moment when he can no longer hold back. His release comes in a series of powerful waves, his groan vibrating through the air, low and raw. The water ripples with the force of it, and I watch, fascinated and breathless, as his seed mixes with the water, settling on my hands and skin.

For a moment, neither of us speaks. His chest heaves as he catches his breath, his dark eyes meeting mine with an intensity that makes my heart stutter. His lips curve into a slow, satisfied smile, and he reaches out to brush a strand of wet hair from my face. "That," he says softly, his voice warm and full of something I can't quite name, "is the best sight I've ever seen."

His words make my cheeks burn, but there's no mockery in his tone, only sincerity. I glance down at my hands, still slick with his release, and something about the sight makes my chest tighten. It's intimate, overwhelming, and yet… not unpleasant.

Without thinking, I lift my hand to my lips, hesitating for just a moment before tasting the faint saltiness left on my fingers. It's an impulsive act, one born of curiosity and something deeper I don't fully understand. When I glance back at him, his eyes darken, the red ring around his pupils glowing brighter.

"You'll be the death of me," he murmurs, his voice thick with heat. His hand moves to my chin, tilting my face up to his. "Do you even realize what you're doing to me?"

I don't know how to answer. My body is still buzzing, my mind racing, and all I can do is stare up at him, caught in the weight of his gaze. Before I can think too much, his lips are on mine, firm and commanding. The kiss is deep, unyielding, claiming me in a way that leaves no room for hesitation. My hands slide up to his shoulders, gripping tightly as I lean into him, letting the warmth of his touch drown out everything else.

As his hands move over me, spreading the remnants of his release across my skin with slow, deliberate strokes, I shiver under his touch. It feels intimate in a way I've never known, his fingers tracing patterns on my arms, my thighs, my stomach. He's marking me, not just with his hands but with every ounce of his presence, his power.

When he finally shifts to stand, the water cascades down his body, glistening against his dark skin. I watch him, breathless, as he steps out of the tub, his movements unhurried but deliberate.

"Come," he says softly, holding out a hand. "Let me take care of you now."

His words are a promise, and as I take his hand, I realize I trust him to keep it.

He pulls me to my feet, the warmth of his body radiating even as the cooler air of the room brushes against my damp skin.

Before I can speak, he wraps a thick, soft towel around me, his hands quick and efficient as he secures it. Then, without a word, he grabs another towel for himself, draping it around his waist before leaning down to drain the tub. The sound of the water swirling away fills the quiet, but my eyes are fixed on him, on the way his movements seem so sure, so steady.

When he straightens, he turns back to me, his gaze softer now. His hands are gentle as he dries me off, the towel brushing over my skin in slow, deliberate strokes. There's a care in his actions that makes my chest ache, a quiet reverence I hadn't expected but can feel in every touch. When he's done, he drops the towel on top of his clothing and takes my hand, leading me toward the cot.

The furs are warm and inviting as he pulls me down beside him, his strong arms wrapping around me as he settles me against his chest. I can hear the steady beat of his heart beneath my ear, a rhythm that calms the lingering tension in my body. His scent wraps around me, grounding me in the moment.

His hand strokes softly over my back, his fingers tracing idle patterns that make my skin tingle. "I can survive whatever this realm requires of me," he murmurs, his voice low and full of quiet conviction, "as long as you're here to stay."

His words settle over me like a fur, warm and reassuring, and I feel my chest tighten with emotions I can't yet name. I press closer to him, my hand resting lightly on his chest as I let his heartbeat lull me into a sense of peace I haven't felt in so long.

"I'm here," I whisper, my voice barely audible, but I know he hears me. "I'm not going anywhere."

His arms tighten around me, pulling me closer, and for the first time in what feels like forever, I feel completely safe. Completely his.

CHAPTER SEVEN

The dining room is alive with quiet conversation this morning, the clink of utensils against plates blending with the occasional soft laughter. Despite the hum of activity, the air feels heavy, charged with unspoken tension. I try to focus on the faces around the table, familiar and comforting, but my gaze keeps drifting toward Rhadis.

He sits next to me at the head of the table, his presence as commanding as ever, though I can see the weight he's carrying. His dark eyes are sharp, his posture rigid, but there's a heaviness in the way he moves, a subtle tightness in his jaw that only I seem to notice. I rest my hand lightly on his, my fingers curling around his as if to silently remind him that I'm here.

Across the table, Fenor catches my eye, his expression steady but questioning, silently asking if I'm all right. I offer him a small nod and smile before turning my attention back to Rhadis as he begins to speak.

"The situation yesterday," he starts, his voice low but cutting through the chatter with ease, "was an escape from one of the prisons. Eight prisoners broke free—six shifters and two Lakin."

The room quiets immediately, all attention snapping to him. His tone is calm, measured, but I can see the faint twitch in his fingers where they rest under my own on the table.

"Two Wolfers, two Cayman, one Tecan, and one Dragon," he continues, his words precise. "The Lakin were highly skilled in illusion, which made them the most dangerous of the group."

A murmur ripples through the table. I glance at Emory, who is sitting beside Ryat, her brow furrowed in thought. Rhadis's grip on my hand tightens slightly, and I glance up at him, my heart twisting at the strain I see in his expression.

"They broke free of the southern prison," he explains, his fingers tapping lightly against the edge of the table. "I had to deal with them personally. Battling them all ensured their bodies would return to the prisons—their final resting place within the underworld."

His voice tightens slightly, and I can hear the strain beneath his calm exterior. "It takes a lot of effort to contain them when there's an escape. Even for me."

"When a person dies, their body is brought to the underworld, where it is sorted," he says, his voice quieter now but no less commanding. "Those who lived good lives are sent to peaceful grounds or villages, where they can reunite with loved ones who have passed. But dark souls—those who lived with malice—are sent to one of the four prisons."

The room is completely silent, every pair of eyes fixed on him. I can feel the tension thickening, the weight of his words settling over everyone like a heavy fur.

"The eight who escaped yesterday have been returned to their cells," Rhadis continues. "The jailers will keep a closer watch on them, ensuring they are kept apart. But the hardest part of maintaining the underworld is managing the prisoners' gifts. They don't lose them in death, and even I can't take them away."

His voice tightens, and I feel his hand tremble slightly under mine. The room is heavy with silence as everyone absorbs Rhadis's words. I shift slightly in my seat, reaching up to rest my other hand gently on his arm. "You handled it," I say softly, keeping my voice steady despite the emotions swirling inside me. "And you'll handle it again if you have to."

He glances at me, his dark eyes meeting mine, and for a moment, the hard edges of his expression soften. A flicker of gratitude lights in his gaze, faint but unmistakable, and it steadies something in me. Even without words, the connection between us feels unshakable. I squeeze his arm gently, letting him know I'm here, that I see the weight he carries even when he doesn't want to show it.

He nods, the faintest hint of relief tugging at his features, and my chest tightens. I know how much he carries—how much he's always carried—and I'll stand beside him no matter how heavy the burden becomes.

The murmured conversations around the table slowly start again, the tension easing as Fenor leans forward to ask a question about the jailers. I barely register the words, my focus lingering on Rhadis. His shoulders are still tense, his fingers brushing against the edge of the table absently, as if even in stillness, his mind is restless.

The underworld, the prisons, the sheer weight of his responsibilities—it's more than any one person should have to bear. And yet, he does it.

Every day.

Without faltering.

How he carries it all without breaking is something I've often wondered since we were young. But I know him well enough to see the cracks, the moments where he lets his guard slip just enough for me to glimpse the toll it takes.

I glance at him again, his profile sharp and imposing, and yet there's a quiet vulnerability in the way he leans into my touch. It's fleeting, but it's there, and it makes my resolve even stronger. No matter what, I'll make sure he doesn't carry this alone.

My chest aches at the sight of him carrying this burden, but before I can speak, Emory does.

"Do you wish their gifts could be removed?" she asks softly, her voice cutting through the heavy silence.

Rhadis turns to her, his gaze sharp but thoughtful. "It would make the prisons more manageable," he admits. "But no one has ever been able to remove gifts. They're tied to the soul."

Emory straightens slightly, brushing her fingers over Layken's fur. "I can remove them," she says, her voice calm but firm. "I'm a null."

The air in the room shifts instantly, all eyes snapping to her. Rhadis stiffens beside me, his dark eyes narrowing slightly as he studies her. I know he is aware of this from his notes, so I wonder what has him tensing.

"I wasn't always in control of it," Emory continues, her voice steady despite the weight of the attention on her. "But Ymir trained me. I don't need touch anymore. I can strip someone's gifts with just a thought."

The silence around the table is deafening. I glance at Fenor, whose expression is unreadable, though I can see the tension in his jaw. Nox, sitting across from me, looks deeply troubled as he studies the table.

"Ymir trained you?" Rhadis asks, his voice low, carrying a sharp edge.

Emory nods, her gaze dropping slightly. "On prisoners at the homestead," she admits quietly. We all know she wants to add that she had little choice, hell, nobody knows that better than me I suppose. I didn't have a choice either.

I see Rhadis's jaw tighten, a flicker of anger flashing across his face, but he doesn't speak. Instead, Arden leans forward, his voice soft but insistent. "How did you get past the fear, Emory?" he asks. "You used to be terrified of your gifts. Of touch."

Emory blinks at him, her brow furrowing. "I don't remember that," she says, her voice faltering. "When I woke up without my memories, the fear was just... gone. There was only curiosity and a need to understand my gifts."

The tension around the table is palpable, and I can feel Rhadis's anger simmering beside me. Before anyone else can speak, Emory turns back to him.

"If you want their gifts gone," she says, her voice stronger now, "I can do it. There are very few gifts I don't already have by now."

Rhadis watches her closely, his gaze sharp and assessing. "Would you be willing to take on the burden of so many gifts?" he asks, his voice quiet but weighted.

Emory smiles faintly, a spark of determination in her eyes. "It wouldn't be much of a burden," she says lightly. "And besides, I don't have a dragon shifter form yet. That sounds… exciting."

A flicker of amusement crosses Rhadis's face, though his expression remains mostly serious. "It's not about power," he says. "It's about control. Carrying gifts like those requires an unshakable will."

"I know," Emory replies simply. "And I can handle it."

The room falls into a heavy silence again before Rhadis nods. "We'll discuss it later."

The conversation shifts, the tension easing slightly, but my thoughts linger on what was just said. As everyone finishes eating and begins to disperse, I glance at Rhadis, his hand still in mine, and feel the weight of his burdens. He's strong—stronger than anyone I've ever known—but even the strongest need someone to hold them up. And I'm here for him. Always.

The clatter of chairs echoes softly as everyone leaves the dining room, the meal over and the morning settling into its usual rhythm. I gather myself to follow, my hand brushing lightly against Rhadis's arm as we rise together, but before we can leave, Holic steps into the room.

His presence is sharp and deliberate, and I instantly know whatever he's come to deliver isn't good news. Rhadis notices too, his gaze narrowing as he pauses and then slowly sinks back into his chair.

"Speak," Rhadis commands, his tone clipped but steady, the authority in his voice leaving no room for delay.

Holic approaches, his movements precise as he bows slightly and hands Rhadis a folded parchment. "A message, my lord," Holic says. His voice is calm, but there's a tension in his movements, a stiffness that speaks volumes.

Rhadis unfolds the parchment, his expression unreadable as his dark eyes scan the words. The air around him seems to shift, growing heavier with each passing second, and I step closer, unable to stop myself from leaning over his shoulder to see what it says.

The words blur together at first, but then my eyes catch on a name that makes my blood run cold.

Ymir.

I freeze, my breath catching in my throat as I read the rest of the message. It's from one of the servants Rhadis has stationed as a watch over Ymir, and the report is grim. Ymir is in Frontasia, his rage palpable even through the written words. Worse, the note says he's moving closer to the entrance of the underworld.

"He's looking for a way in," I whisper, my voice barely audible as my eyes dart over the rest of the note. "Rhadis, he's..."

"I see it," Rhadis cuts in, his voice low and dangerous, the calm veneer cracking just enough to reveal the storm beneath. He sets the parchment on the table, his fingers tapping against the wood as he stares at the words.

"Frontasia," he mutters, the name laced with disdain. "That's closer than I expected."

"Too close," I add, my heart pounding as I straighten, my hands gripping the back of his chair. "He'll try to use the entrance to get to Emory, to her child. You know he will."

Rhadis's jaw tightens, his expression hardening into the sharp, unyielding mask he wears when his control is tested. "If he steps foot near the underworld, I'll deal with him," he says, his tone cold and final.

"But he's already close," I press, my voice rising slightly with urgency. "We can't wait for him to reach the entrance. We have to stop him now."

He glances up at me, his dark eyes meeting mine, and for a moment, there's a flicker of something softer there. "I will handle it, Raya," he says, his voice quieter now, but no less resolute. "I won't let him come near you. Or them."

The room feels too quiet now, the weight of the conversation pressing down on me like a stone. I look back at the parchment, the jagged lines of the servant's hurried writing seeming to pulse with the gravity of the situation.

"What are you going to do?" I ask, my voice steady despite the fear tightening in my chest.

Rhadis stands, his presence towering as he folds the parchment and tucks it into his coat. "What I must," he says simply, his voice devoid of doubt. He glances at Holic. "Prepare my things. I leave within the hour."

The room is suffocatingly silent as Rhadis sets the parchment on the table, his jaw tight and his fingers tapping a steady rhythm against the wood. I lean closer, my eyes scanning the words again as my heart hammers in my chest.

"He's getting closer to the entrance," I say, my voice sharp with worry. "Rhadis, you can't go alone."

"I will handle this," he replies, his tone cold and resolute. "You're staying here. It's too dangerous."

"No," I say immediately, stepping closer to him, my hand gripping the back of his chair. "I'm coming with you."

His head snaps up, his dark eyes narrowing as they meet mine. "Raya, no," he says firmly. "This isn't up for debate. Your safety is —"

"My safety is always your first concern," I interrupt, my voice rising. "But what about you? You think I'm just going to sit here while you face Ymir alone? What if something happens? What if —"

"Nothing will happen," he says, his voice dropping an octave, though it's not as reassuring as he seems to think. "I've dealt with him before. I know how to handle him."

"But he's different now," I argue, stepping closer, my chest tight with frustration and fear. "He's more dangerous than ever, and I can help you."

"Raya," he says, his voice softening, though his expression remains hard. "You've already risked too much for me. I can't let you—"

"This isn't just about you," I snap, cutting him off again. "This is about Emory and my brother and everyone else who depends on you. You need someone by your side, someone who knows how to fight, someone you trust. And you trust me."

His lips press into a thin line, his jaw ticking as he stares at me. I can see the war waging behind his eyes, the need to keep me safe battling with the truth of my words. Finally, he exhales sharply, running a hand through his hair.

"If you come with me," he says, his voice low and tense, "you listen to me. No arguments, no disobedience. When I tell you to do something, you do it. Understood?"

I nod, relief washing over me even as my heart pounds. "Understood."

He steps closer, his hands gripping my shoulders as his dark eyes bore into mine. "I'm serious, Raya. If you put yourself in danger, if you defy me—"

"I won't," I promise, my voice steady despite the swirling emotions inside me. "I'll listen. But I'm not staying behind."

He studies me for a long moment before nodding, his grip on my shoulders relaxing slightly. "Fine," he mutters. "But don't make me regret this."

"You won't," I say softly, though the knot of fear in my stomach doesn't ease.

Rhadis turns to Holic, who has been standing silently nearby, and gives him a curt nod. "Prepare supplies for two. We leave within the hour."

Holic bows and slips out of the room, leaving us alone. Rhadis turns back to me, his expression still tense. "Go get ready," he says, his voice quieter now. "And remember what you promised."

I nod again, stepping back reluctantly before turning toward the door. My mind is already racing with preparations, but as I glance back at him, still standing at the head of the table, I can't help but feel a pang of worry. He's strong, but even the strongest need help sometimes. And I'll be damned if I let him face this alone.

CHAPTER EIGHT

I pace around the room, packing a bag with everything I think we might need, though I have no idea what to expect. A few furs, a flask of water, and a pillow are all tucked inside, though I hesitate over a small blade resting on the dresser. After a moment, I grab it and slide it into the bag, just in case.

My mind spins as I move, thoughts of what lies ahead twisting into knots of anxiety and determination. Ymir is too close to the underworld, too dangerous, and I can't stand the thought of Rhadis going after him alone. I cinch the bag shut with trembling hands and set it by the door, just as I hear his heavy footsteps approaching.

The door swings open, and Rhadis steps inside, his tall frame filling the space effortlessly. He looks over me and then the bag, his dark eyes narrowing slightly. "Are you sure you're ready for this?" he asks, his tone firm but not unkind. "You know what we're walking into, don't you?"

I straighten, meeting his gaze. "I'm ready," I say without

hesitation, though my heart races. "And yes, I know it won't be easy. That's why I'm going."

He exhales sharply, rubbing a hand over his jaw as he studies me. "You aren't exactly known for your obedience, Raya," he says, his tone edged with wry amusement despite the tension in the room. "What makes you think you can handle this without getting us both killed?"

I fold my arms, tilting my head at him. "Maybe that's because your 'commands' tend to be unreasonable," I retort, my voice light but pointed. "If you're fair, I'll listen."

His lips twitch into a faint smirk, though his dark eyes remain serious. "Fair, huh?" he murmurs, stepping closer. "You think you'll be the one to decide what's fair?"

"I always have," I reply, lifting my chin. "You knew that about me as a child, and it hasn't changed."

His smirk fades into something softer, though his gaze remains sharp. "You're infuriating," he mutters, reaching out to brush a strand of hair from my face. "But I'd rather have you with me than leave you here worrying."

"Good," I say firmly, my hand brushing his as I adjust the strap of the bag. "Because I wasn't going to stay behind."

His hand lingers on my cheek for a moment, his touch warm and grounding. "You don't make anything easy," he murmurs, though there's no heat in the words. "Just... remember what I said. When I tell you to do something, you do it. No arguing."

I nod, though the corner of my mouth twitches into a slight

smile. “I’ll try my best,” I say, unable to resist the jab.

He shakes his head, his dark hair falling slightly into his face. “Trouble,” he mutters, though there’s a flicker of affection in his eyes as he steps back. “Grab your things. Holic is waiting for us.”

I pick up the bag, my heart pounding as I follow him out of the room. The weight of what’s ahead looms over us, but for the first time in a long while, I feel ready. No matter what comes, I’ll be by his side. And I won’t let him face it alone.

The world swirls around me, a rush of Rhadis’s magic that feels like a mixture of shadows and heat. It isn’t unpleasant—if anything, it feels strangely familiar and grounding—but it leaves me momentarily disoriented. When my feet touch solid ground again, I blink my eyes open and let out a soft gasp.

The forest before us is unlike anything I’ve ever seen. The trees are vibrant, their leaves shimmering in hues of emerald, gold, and fiery orange. Bright flowers bloom in clusters along the path, their petals swaying gently in the breeze, and the air smells of earth and wild sweetness. It’s breathtaking, and for a moment, I forget the reason we’re here.

“Welcome to Frontasia,” Rhadis murmurs, his voice pulling me back to reality.

I glance over at him, taking in his steady expression and the four heavy bags slung effortlessly over his broad shoulders. Holic is gone, and I realize it’s just the two of us now. My heart tightens at the thought.

He reaches out. “Hand me your bag,” he says simply.

I blink at him, gripping the strap of my bag tighter. "I can carry it," I argue, frowning at him. "You're already carrying too much."

He quirks a brow at me, his expression somewhere between amused and annoyed. "Raya," he says, his tone patient but firm, "give me the bag."

"It's just furs and water!" I protest, lifting the bag slightly as if to prove how light it is. "I'm perfectly capable of carrying it."

"You are," he agrees, nodding. "But you don't need to. I've got it."

I let out a frustrated sigh, my grip tightening on the strap. "You're impossible," I mutter, but I know I'm not going to win this argument. With a reluctant groan, I shove the bag toward him. "Fine. Take it."

He takes it without a word, tossing it over his shoulder as if it weighs nothing. His smirk is barely contained, and I glare at him as we start walking.

The forest path is soft beneath our boots, and for a while, the only sounds are the crunch of leaves and the distant calls of birds. Despite my frustration with Rhadis, I can't stop my gaze from wandering. The woods are stunning, alive with color and light, and yet… something feels off.

Most of the trees are as vibrant as the stories I've heard of Frontasia, their bark rich and full of life. But some of them—scattered here and there—stand in stark contrast. Their trunks are gray and cracked, and black veins crawl up from their bases like an infection. Even their leaves hang limp, dull and lifeless compared to the brilliance around them.

"Are those trees diseased?" I ask, stopping to examine one of the withered trunks. My fingers hover over the black veins, not daring to touch them.

Rhadis stops beside me, his gaze following mine. "No," he says after a moment, his voice low and steady. "They're suffering from the curse."

I look up at him, confused. "The curse on the lands? Like the report in your letter?"

He nods, his jaw tightening. "It affects more than just people," he explains. "The earth, the trees, even the animals—everything is connected. The curse eats away at them, poisoning the roots and leeching the life from the ground. These trees will continue to wither and die unless it's broken."

My chest tightens as I look back at the tree, the black veins seeming even darker now. "How do we stop it?" I ask softly, though I already know the answer.

He doesn't respond right away, his eyes fixed on the deadened bark. "We break the curse," he says finally, his voice heavy with the weight of it. "And that means stopping Ymir."

The words hang in the air between us, stark and unyielding. I reach out and brush my fingers lightly over the bark, the rough texture sending a shiver up my spine. The tree feels hollow, almost as if it's already gone.

"Let's keep moving," Rhadis says, his voice softer now but still resolute.

I nod, tearing my gaze away from the tree as we continue down the path. The forest feels different now, the beauty around me tainted by the knowledge of what lies beneath it. And as I glance at Rhadis, his strong, determined figure walking ahead of me, I wonder how much more we'll have to sacrifice before this curse is finally lifted.

Rhadis stops abruptly, turning to glance back at me. "We'll make camp here," he says, his voice even and calm.

I look around, noting the small clearing surrounded by thick, vibrant trees, though a few of them show the telltale black veins of the curse. It's quiet here, the air cool and still, and I can see why he chose it. He sets the five bags down with ease, barely winded despite the distance we've walked.

Before I can say anything, he reaches into one of the bags and pulls out a flask, handing it to me. "Drink," he commands, his tone brooking no argument.

I raise an eyebrow but take the flask, unscrewing the cap and sipping the cool water. He watches me closely, arms crossed over his chest, until I've taken several gulps. "Satisfied?" I ask, handing it back to him.

"Not yet," he replies, his lips quirking in the faintest of smirks before he turns to the pile of bags and begins unpacking.

I watch as he works quickly, pulling out stakes and fabric and laying them on the ground. He's quiet, focused, and for a moment, I just stand there, unsure of how to help. But when he starts hammering stakes into the ground to build what looks like the saddest excuse for a tent I've ever seen, I can't help but laugh.

"Is this really your idea of a tent?" I tease, crossing my arms. "I expected more from the God of the Underworld."

He glances up at me, one eyebrow raised. "Oh, ye of little faith," he says dryly, standing back and brushing the dirt from his hands. The tent looks barely functional, sagging slightly on one side, and I suppress another laugh as he steps toward it.

"Watch," he says, his voice soft, almost a command.

Before I can question him, I see it—shadows trailing out of his skin like ink, winding their way into the fabric of the tent. My breath catches as the shadows spread, shifting and swirling until the structure begins to change. The thin fabric solidifies, stretching and growing, and within moments, the sad little tent has been replaced by a small, sleek black cabin.

I stare, wide-eyed, as he steps back and gestures toward the cabin with a faint smirk. "Satisfied now?"

"How did you...?" I trail off, taking a step closer to the cabin and running my fingers over the smooth, cool surface. "How did you do that?"

He shrugs, brushing his hands off again. "My powers allow me to control the underworld, and in some ways, they make it a part of me," he explains. "As long as there's a structure already in place, like that tent, I can swap it for one of the homes within the underworld."

I turn to him, frowning slightly. "But... What about the people who lived in the home you replaced it with? Won't they need it?"

He shakes his head. "This one wasn't in use. I'd never take a home from someone who needed it."

His words ease the faint worry in my chest, and I nod, stepping closer to the cabin. It's small—much smaller than our room back at his castle—but it's cozy. A cot rests against one wall, positioned across from a small hearth that I assume will serve as a fireplace. Two chairs sit near a counter in the corner that looks like it could be used as a kitchen space. It's simple but inviting, and I can already imagine curling up by the hearth when the night gets colder.

I glance around, noting a small door tucked into one corner of the cabin. Curiosity pulls me toward it, and I open it to find a tiny outhouse—an actual place to use the bathroom. Relief washes over me, and I can't help but smile as I turn back to Rhadis.

"You've officially exceeded my expectations," I tell him, grinning. "I was worried I'd have to use the bushes."

He chuckles softly, setting the last of the bags on the counter. "I wouldn't subject you to that," he says, his tone light. "Even I'm not that cruel."

I laugh, shaking my head as I step back into the main room. The cabin may be small, but it already feels like a safe haven. As I glance around again, my gaze catches on Rhadis, his dark presence somehow fitting perfectly in the cozy space. And for a moment, I let myself relax, knowing that no matter what lies ahead, I'll face it with him by my side.

Rhadis leans back against the counter, his sharp gaze following me as I adjust the last few items in the cabin. He crosses his arms, his expression softening ever so slightly as his eyes flicker over me. "You look like you could use a rest," he says, his voice low but warm. "Are you tired? It's almost dark."

I turn to him, smiling at the concern in his tone. "No," I reply, shaking my head. "I'm fine. But... if you don't mind, I was thinking about stretching my legs a bit."

His brows knit together in confusion. "The hike wasn't long enough for that?" he asks, tilting his head slightly.

I suppress a laugh, my smile widening as I step closer to him. "Not quite," I say, lowering a hand to the top of my short traveling dress. His eyes narrow slightly as I tug at the ties, loosening them until the fabric falls just enough to bare my chest.

Rhadis grumbles something under his breath, the sound a deep rumble that sends a shiver down my spine. He steps forward, his hands twitching at his sides, as I glance up at him with a teasing smile. "This form's legs aren't the ones I wish to stretch," I say softly, my voice laced with amusement.

His lips twitch into a faint smirk, though the red rings around his pupils pulse brightly, betraying the heat in his gaze. "Are you stripping just to tease me?" he asks, his voice rougher now, edged with both amusement and frustration.

"Maybe," I say with a soft giggle, letting the dress slip further until it pools at my feet. I stand before him, completely bare, my skin prickling under his intense gaze.

His hand moves before I can process it, reaching out to touch me. His fingers hover just above my skin, his restraint evident, though the flicker of fire in his eyes shows how much effort it takes. "You're impossible," he mutters, his voice low and almost reverent.

I laugh again, stepping back as the familiar pull of my shift ripples through me. "Don't blink," I tease, the sensation of my body changing taking hold. My bones twist and reshape, my skin prickling as soft copper fur grows over it. My senses sharpen, my vision and hearing growing clearer as my form shifts completely.

When the transformation is complete, I shake out my body, stretching my legs and tail with a luxurious arch of my back. I look up at him, now from a lower angle, and let out a soft chirp. My fluffy copper fur glints faintly in the cabin's dim light, and I swish my tail as I move closer to him.

Rhadis lets out a low laugh, crouching to meet my eyes. "A 20-pound menace," he murmurs, his tone full of warmth and exasperation. "Should've guessed it'd be a Silken, you did love them as a child."

I purr in response, rubbing against his leg as he reaches out to stroke my fur. His fingers are gentle, tracing over my back and shoulders, and I push into his touch, letting the vibrations of my purr deepen.

"You're lucky you're cute," he says, his smirk softening as he watches me with a mixture of affection and amusement. "And here I thought you wanted to stretch your legs. Not run circles around me."

I let out a small chirp again, padding toward the door, my tail swishing behind me. I glance back at him with a playful glint in my eyes before darting out of the cabin and into the forest. I don't need to look back to know he's following—I can hear the soft curse under his breath as he grabs his coat and steps out after me.

The cold forest air rushes through my fur as I leap onto a nearby rock, my claws scratching against the stone for balance. Freedom surges through me, a thrilling reminder of the joy in shifting, and for a moment, all thoughts of curses and danger melt away.

The forest is alive with the muted whispers of winter, the chill in the air brushing against my fur as I dart between the trees. Small patches of snow dot the ground, scattered like fragments of clouds fallen from the sky. My silken form, lightweight and nimble, carries me effortlessly, but I'm careful to avoid the damp patches of melting snow. This body doesn't appreciate wet paws, and I let out a small huff as I leap over a particularly large patch.

The crisp air carries the faintest scent of pine and frost, mingled with the earthy richness of the forest floor. My whiskers twitch as I pick up faint sounds—the rustle of leaves, the distant snap of a twig. The world feels sharper, more vibrant in this form, and I revel in the thrill of it.

Spotting a sturdy tree ahead, I gather my strength and leap, my claws digging into the bark as I climb. The branches sway slightly under my weight, but I find my balance easily, settling onto a wide limb. From this height, the view is breathtaking—bare branches weaving an intricate canopy against the pale sky, the vibrant greens and whites of the forest blending in a chaotic harmony.

Below me, Rhadis waits, his tall form a dark contrast against the lighter surroundings. Shadows swirl faintly at his feet, as though they can't quite contain themselves, and I pause for a moment, watching him. Even now, even in this form, I can't help but notice how striking he is. The strength in his stance, the way his eyes glint as he looks up at me—he's beautiful in a way that feels both otherworldly and achingly real.

I swish my tail, batting at a dry leaf caught in the tree beside me. It flutters downward, catching the wind, and I follow its descent with idle curiosity before finally making my way down the trunk. My claws scrape lightly against the bark as I touch down on the ground, and the moment my paws hit the forest floor, Rhadis is there.

He scoops me up effortlessly, his strong arms cradling my smaller form against his chest. His warmth seeps through my fur, a welcome contrast to the chill of the air, and I let out a soft purr as he scratches under my chin.

"You've had your fun," he murmurs, his voice low and full of warmth. "But I'd like to get you out of the cold now."

I nuzzle into him, my purr deepening as his fingers find the spot behind my ears. The shadows that cling to him seem to settle slightly, drawn in by his steady presence, and I can't help but relax against him. He strokes the soft fur along my back as he begins walking, his long strides carrying us swiftly through the forest and back toward the cabin.

The sounds of the forest fade as we approach the small black structure. Rhadis opens the door without setting me down, his movements fluid. Inside, the warmth of the cabin wraps around us, and I stretch slightly in his arms, feeling safe and content.

"You're trouble, you know that?" he says softly, his lips quirking into a faint smirk as he scratches behind my ears again. But his tone holds no reprimand—only affection.

I nuzzle against his chest, my purr vibrating through me as I let myself sink into the comfort of his touch. For now, the rest of the world can wait.

CHAPTER NINE

The soft hum of Rhadis's breathing pulls me from the haze of sleep. The warmth of his skin beneath me is steady and grounding, and for a moment, I don't move, content to let the quiet surround us. I stretch slightly, my fluffy copper tail curling against his side, and settle again, the comfort of my Silken form soothing the lingering edges of my dreams.

I know I should shift back, should greet the day in my normal form and face whatever lies ahead. But I don't. The feel of this form, the familiarity of it, keeps me rooted. There's a strange kind of peace in it—a connection to something simpler, even if that connection isn't entirely by choice.

My thoughts drift, unbidden, to a time I try not to think about. Back to the potion. Back to the lord who forced it on me without a second thought. I can still taste the bitterness of it, can still feel the suffocating trap of being locked in this form, unable to shift back.

I was just a plaything for his son. An "adorable little pet," as the boy called me. The lord didn't care that I hated it, didn't care that my fur felt suffocating after weeks, months, of being stuck. I was a servant—my opinions didn't matter.

My freedom didn't matter.

The memory of my brother finding me like that flashes through my mind, sharp and painful. He didn't recognize me at first. How could he? I was just a silken—a silent, desperate silken unable to speak or explain. His confusion turned to anger when he realized that the scent of his sister was in fact coming from me, and I'll never forget the look in his eyes when he promised to fix it. He and Dyra found the potion, the one that made it possible for me to shift back, and the relief of being normal again was indescribable. But something had shifted in me after that. My regular form felt foreign, unfamiliar, like a piece of me had been left behind in that cage.

Even now, months later, I can't shake that feeling entirely. This form, my silken form, feels like a second skin—sometimes more natural than the one I was born with.

A soft murmur pulls me from my thoughts. Rhadis shifts beneath me, his hand moving to rest gently against my back. His warmth seeps through my fur, and I glance up to see his dark eyes blinking open, the red ring around his pupils faint but still present.

"What are you thinking about?" he asks, his voice low and rough with sleep. His fingers stroke along my spine, the touch so tender it makes my chest ache.

I hesitate, curling my tail tighter against him. For a moment, I think about staying silent, about letting the past stay buried where it belongs. But the way he looks at me, the steady patience in his gaze, unravels something in me.

I shift, the transformation rippling through me with a familiar pull. My fur recedes, my bones rearranging, until I'm left naked in his arms, my skin warm against his. He doesn't flinch, doesn't look away, just waits, his hand still resting on my back as if to reassure me.

"It was a long time ago," I start, my voice quiet, almost hesitant. "Before Ymir. Before Dyra found me."

He doesn't interrupt, his gaze steady and calm as I take a breath and continue.

"The lord I worked for… he made me drink a potion," I say, my fingers gripping the edge of the furs. "It locked me in my Silken form. His son… he thought it was fun to have a 'pet.' And since I was just a servant, what I wanted didn't matter."

Rhadis's hand tightens slightly on my back, his jaw clenching. He doesn't speak, but the weight of his anger is palpable, not directed at me but at the memory I'm recounting.

"My brother found me like that," I say, my voice breaking slightly. "Stuck. Silent. I couldn't even tell him why I was stuck like that. It took him and Dyra weeks to find a potion to reverse it."

"And they did," Rhadis says, his voice low and steady, though there's an edge to it, as though he's barely containing his rage. "They got you out."

I nod, swallowing hard. "They did. But… I don't know. After

being stuck that way for so long, my human form didn't feel the same. Sometimes it still doesn't."

His other hand comes up, brushing a strand of hair from my face. "Raya," he murmurs, his voice softening. "You're not there anymore. You're here. With me."

I look up at him, my chest tightening at the raw honesty in his gaze. "I know," I whisper. "But it doesn't make the memories go away."

"No," he agrees, his thumb brushing lightly along my jaw. "But you don't have to carry them alone."

Something in his words eases the tightness in my chest, and I let out a shaky breath, leaning into his touch. For the first time in a long while, I feel like maybe he's right. Maybe I don't have to carry it all by myself.

Rhadis's fingers stroke along my skin, the slow and deliberate movement sending shivers up my spine. His touch is gentle at first, soothing, as if he's trying to ease the tension from my body after everything I've just shared. But then his hand trails lower, brushing the curve of my waist, his thumb grazing the soft skin just beneath my breast.

I tense for a moment, unprepared for the boldness of the gesture, but the warmth in his eyes holds me steady. He's watching me, reading every shift in my expression, and the care in his gaze makes my chest ache in a way I don't know how to name.

His hand moves again, fingers skimming over the peak of my breast, brushing lightly over my nipple. I gasp softly, the sensation unfamiliar and yet... not unwelcome. Heat blooms low in my belly, and I feel my skin flush as he circles my nipple with his thumb, his touch both firm and teasing.

"You're beautiful," he murmurs, his voice low and rough. His other hand slides down, trailing over the curve of my hip to rest on my ass, squeezing gently.

I bite my lip, my mind spinning. His touch feels good—more than good—but it's the contrast to everything I've known before that leaves me reeling. I've had hands on me before, sure. Most servants do. Lords and their guests don't ask permission, don't care how we feel. We're just another thing they own. Another thing to use.

But this is different. This is... mine. This is him. Rhadis doesn't take. He waits. He gives. And it's the giving that shakes me, that surprises me, that makes me realize how much I like his touch. How much I want more of it.

"You're quiet," he says, his tone almost teasing, though there's a softness in his expression. "Should I stop?"

"No," I blurt out before I can stop myself, my voice breathless and raw. My cheeks burn, and I glance away, embarrassed by the need in my tone. "I mean... no. You don't have to stop."

His lips quirk into a faint smile, and his hand on my ass tightens slightly, pulling me closer. "Good," he says, his voice dropping an octave as his thumb brushes over my nipple again. "Because I don't want to."

I shiver, my body betraying me as it arches into his touch. The heat in his gaze only intensifies, and I feel my breath hitch as his hand trails lower, skimming over the curve of my thigh.

"You're so responsive," he murmurs, almost to himself, his eyes darkening as he watches me. "I like that."

My heart pounds in my chest, my mind struggling to keep up with the sensations coursing through me. This isn't like anything I've ever known. It's slower, deeper, more intentional. He's not just touching me—he's learning me, exploring me, as though every inch of my skin is something to be discovered.

"I..." My voice falters, and I swallow hard, trying to gather my thoughts. "I'm not used to this."

He pauses, his hand stilling on my skin as his gaze meets mine. "Not used to what?" he asks softly, his tone gentle but curious.

"To... wanting this," I admit, my voice barely above a whisper. "To someone touching me like this."

His expression softens, the intensity in his eyes giving way to something warmer, something achingly tender. "You deserve to be touched like this," he says, his voice low but steady. "You deserve to be wanted, to feel good. And I'll show you everything, if you let me."

My throat tightens, emotions swirling inside me that I don't know how to name. But I nod, the smallest of movements, and his smile deepens, his hand resuming its exploration.

For the first time, I let myself feel without questioning it. Let myself enjoy the weight of his hand on my skin, the warmth of his touch, the way his fingers seem to know exactly where to linger. And for the first time, it feels like something I'm allowed to want.

Something that's mine.

Rhadis's touch is deliberate, his hands skimming over my skin with practiced ease. I shiver as his fingers trail lower, teasing along my thighs. His touch lingers, and then his fingers brush against my sex. My gasp is sharp, echoing softly in the quiet room. It's not the first time he's touched me there, but the sensation still feels startling, overwhelming in its intensity.

He leans in, his lips capturing mine in a kiss that's slow and purposeful, his tongue sweeping past my lips to deepen it. My hands clutch at his shoulders, grounding myself as the heat from his body seems to seep into mine. His fingers stroke gently, teasing, and I feel my body arch toward him, chasing the sensation.

"Rhadis," I whisper against his mouth, my voice trembling. My cheeks flush as I realize how needy I sound, but his low chuckle sends a wave of heat through me.

"You're so beautiful," he murmurs, his voice thick with emotion and desire. His lips move to my jaw, then down to my neck, his kisses slow and lingering as though he's savoring every moment. "You have no idea what you do to me."

The words make my chest tighten, a strange mix of vulnerability and desire flooding through me. Before I can respond, I feel his finger slide inside me, the intrusion slow and careful. A soft gasp escapes me, my fingers tightening on his shoulders as my body reacts instinctively, hips shifting toward his hand.

"You're perfect," he says, his voice a low, soothing hum. His eyes meet mine, glowing faintly with that red ring that always seems more vivid in moments like this. "Just let go, Raya. Let me take care of you."

His words dissolve the last of my hesitation, and I let myself sink into the moment. His finger moves inside me, stroking with deliberate precision, his thumb circling a sensitive spot that sends sparks of pleasure shooting through me. The combination is maddening, a steady build of sensation that leaves me breathless.

"Rhadis," I gasp again, my voice higher now, tinged with desperation. My legs tremble as the pressure in my core builds, tightening with every stroke of his fingers.

"I've got you," he murmurs, his lips brushing against my ear. His free hand cups my face, his thumb stroking my cheek as though to anchor me. "You're incredible, Raya. Every sound you make, every shiver—it's all mine."

The possessiveness in his voice sends another wave of heat through me, and I feel myself tipping over the edge. The pressure bursts, pleasure crashing through me in waves so intense I can't hold back the cry that escapes my lips. My body shakes, every nerve alight, as his fingers continue to stroke me through the aftershocks.

"That's it," he says softly, his voice filled with awe and warmth. "You're breathtaking like this."

I cling to him, my face buried against his chest as I try to catch my breath. His fingers slow, their movements gentle now, coaxing the last tremors of pleasure from me. His other hand moves to my back, rubbing soothing circles as he holds me close.

"You're incredible," he murmurs again, his lips pressing against my temple. The words wrap around me like a warm fur, and for the first time in a long while, I feel completely safe, completely cherished.

CHAPTER TEN

Rhadis's arms tighten around me, his warmth grounding me as I rest against his chest. His fingers trail lazily along my arm, tracing small patterns on my skin, and I can't help but smile, feeling content in a way I haven't felt in years. His breathing is steady, and I close my eyes, letting myself linger in the safety of his embrace.

But soon, he shifts beneath me, and I feel him press a kiss to the top of my head before carefully untangling himself from me. "As much as I'd like to keep you here all day," he murmurs, his deep voice laced with amusement, "we have work to do."

I sit up, watching as he stretches, his broad shoulders rolling back and his arms reaching high above his head. The movement makes his muscles ripple, and the light filtering into the room catches on the ridges and scars of his dark skin. My gaze lingers, heat sparking in my core before I quickly look away, biting my lip.

When I glance back, Rhadis is smiling down at me, a knowing look in his glowing eyes. "Something on your mind, Raya?" he teases, one brow arched.

I shake my head, though my cheeks burn. "Just admiring the view," I admit softly, earning a chuckle from him.

"Well, keep admiring," he says, his grin widening as he offers me a hand to help me up. "But then we need to get started on protecting our realm."

I take his hand, letting him pull me to my feet. The familiar sense of purpose begins to settle over me, though there's still a hint of reluctance to leave the cozy cocoon of our morning together. I stretch my arms overhead, shaking off the lingering warmth of sleep, and glance toward the small counter in the corner.

Rhadis is already ahead of me, pulling out one of the short dresses Helic packed for our travels. He holds it up, examining it with a thoughtful expression before turning to me. "This one," he says, a faint smile playing on his lips. "The green suits you."

I step closer, letting him help me slip it over my head. The fabric is soft, brushing against my skin as he adjusts it on my shoulders. He moves behind me, tugging the laces of the corset tighter until the dress fits snugly against my body. I glance down, noticing how the neckline dips just enough to accentuate my cleavage, and how the hem barely covers my butt in length.

"You just want it tight so you can stare at my cleavage all day," I joke, glancing at him over my shoulder.

He grins unabashedly, his fingers brushing against the small of my back as he ties off the laces. "I won't deny that's a bonus," he says, his tone playful but full of warmth. "And the short hem?

Let's just say it's an added incentive for me to keep close to you today. Who knows, I may even trip—purely by accident, of course—and get a glimpse up my lovely mate's skirt."

I laugh, shaking my head at him. "You're impossible."

"And yet, here you are," he replies, stepping around to face me. His hands settle on my waist, his thumbs brushing the fabric as his gaze roams over me. "You look perfect."

I roll my eyes, though my cheeks flush at the compliment. "Let's see how long you can keep your focus on our mission instead of my legs."

He smirks, his hand drifting to the curve of my hip as he leans in to press a kiss to my forehead. "Challenge accepted."

The forest path stretches ahead, its frosted edges sparkling under the weak winter sunlight. I match Rhadis's stride as best as I can, though his long legs make it difficult to keep up without pushing myself. He glances back every so often, his crimson-ringed eyes scanning the trail ahead and behind, always watching. Always vigilant.

We've been walking for an hour or so when he suddenly stops. I nearly bump into him, blinking in surprise as he shrugs one of the packs off his shoulders and pulls out a fur-lined coat. "Put this on," he says, holding it out to me.

I raise an eyebrow. "I'm fine, Rhadis. It's not even that cold."

His expression doesn't waver, his tone firm as he steps closer. "Humor me."

Sighing, I take the coat from him, the soft fur brushing against my fingers. His gaze doesn't leave me as I slip it on, his hands reaching out to adjust the collar once it's settled over my shoulders.

"There," he says softly, his voice losing some of its edge. "I don't like seeing you uncomfortable, even if you won't admit it."

I roll my eyes, but the warmth that blooms in my chest at his words is undeniable. "You're overprotective, you know that?"

He smirks, shouldering the pack again. "And you wouldn't have it any other way."

The path ahead leads us out of the woods and into a small village nestled at the edge of the trees. Tuinen, he told me earlier —a quiet place with just enough bustle to be considered lively. Smoke rises from homes, and the faint scent of woodsmoke and baked goods hangs in the crisp air. It's quaint, with cobblestone streets and small wooden cabins that look as if they've stood here for centuries.

Rhadis leads me into a diner, the small bell above the door jingling as we step inside. The warmth of the room wraps around me immediately, chasing away the chill from our hike. The smell of frying eggs and freshly brewed coffee fills the air, making my stomach growl despite myself.

We're greeted by a waitress, her face rosy from the heat of the kitchen. She hands us a single sheet of paper each, the menu printed neatly with only six items listed. My eyes scan the options, and my breath catches when I see it.

Sweetberry cakes.

My fingers tighten slightly on the paper as the memory rises unbidden. My mother used to make sweetberry cakes every weekend, the smell of them filling our home, the sticky sweetness lingering on my fingers as I ate them fresh from the skillet. She always smiled as she watched me devour them, telling me they were made with extra love. That memory, one of the few I have of her before I was stolen, feels both sharp and comforting all at once.

"I'll have the sweetberry cakes and a coffee, please," I say quickly, setting the menu down before my voice can waver. I glance at Rhadis, who's watching me with quiet curiosity, and add, "They were… my mother's favorite to make."

His expression softens slightly, but he doesn't say anything, turning to the waitress instead. "Frostbane meat and eggs for me," he says simply.

She nods, scribbling down our order before disappearing into the kitchen.

I lean back in my seat, the rough wood of the chair grounding me as I try to push away the wave of emotion that threatens to overwhelm me. Rhadis reaches across the table, his hand covering mine. His touch is steady, warm, and I find myself anchoring to it.

"Memories like that are worth holding onto," he says quietly, his voice low enough that only I can hear. "Even when they hurt."

I nod, swallowing hard. "I wasn't expecting to see them here," I admit. "It just... caught me off guard."

The waitress returns a few minutes later with our food, and my breath hitches as the plate of sweetberry cakes is set before me. They look almost exactly like the ones my mother used to make, the edges golden and crisp, the berries bursting with color. The smell alone takes me back, and for a moment, I can almost hear her laugh.

I pick up my fork, cutting into the stack and taking a bite. The sweetness floods my senses, and for a brief moment, it feels like I'm home again. Tears prick at the corners of my eyes, but I blink them away quickly, not wanting Rhadis to see. When I glance at him, he's watching me with a faint smile, his plate of meat and eggs barely touched.

"Good?" he asks, his tone light but his gaze serious.

I nod, unable to speak past the lump in my throat. He squeezes my hand once before turning his attention to his own food, giving me the space to process without prying. As we eat, the warm glow of the diner begins to ease the ache that always seems to linger just beneath the surface. The sweetberry cakes remind me of simpler times, but they also stir memories I've kept locked away, ones I've rarely spoken about. With each bite, the weight of those memories presses harder against my chest, until I can't keep them in any longer.

I glance up at Rhadis, his sharp features softened by the flickering candlelight on the table. He's watching me, his attention unwavering, and I realize I don't have to guard myself with him—not here, not now.

"I never thought I'd see them again," I start, my voice quieter than I intended. My fork pauses mid-air, and I stare down at the golden cakes on my plate. "My parents, I mean."

Rhadis doesn't speak, but the way he tilts his head, his gaze softening, invites me to continue.

"When Fenor and the others found me, I'd been stuck in my silken form for years." The words come out sharper than I expect, and I take a deep breath to steady myself. "I didn't think the lord would ever bother looking for me. Why would they? I was a servant, a piece of property to them. But Fenor... he remembered and he had been searching for me. For years. He recognized me."

Rhadis's jaw tightens, but he doesn't interrupt, his hand resting on the table near mine in silent support.

"They brought me back to my parents," I continue, my throat tightening at the memory. "But I couldn't speak to them. Couldn't shift back. I was still stuck as a big cat. My mother cried the moment she saw me, and my father—he just... knelt down and held me, as if he'd known all along that I would come home one day."

My voice wavers, and I grip the edge of the table, trying to hold myself together. "I stayed with them for weeks while Fenor and the group moved on after only a couple days. It was the first real home I'd had since I was there as a child, and even though I couldn't say a word to them, I didn't want to leave."

I glance up at Rhadis, his dark eyes steady on me, his silence a balm rather than a burden. It gives me the strength to keep going.

“Dyra and Fenor came back with the potion,” I say, my voice trembling slightly. “I remember shaking as I drank it, terrified it wouldn’t work. But then… it did. I shifted back. And the first thing I did was throw my arms around my mother and cry like a child.”

The tears I’ve been holding back sting at the corners of my eyes, but I don’t brush them away. “She cried, too. She kept saying my name over and over, as if she couldn’t believe I was real. And my father… he ruffled my hair the way he used to when I was little, when I helped him in the stables.”

I pause, the weight of the memories settling over me like a thick fur. “I’d given up hope of ever seeing them again. I thought if I did, it would mean they’d lost everything—that they’d been dragged into the same life I’d been forced into. But they hadn’t. Their stables, my mothers birthing station—they’d thrived. They’d managed to hold on.”

Rhadis reaches across the table, his hand closing over mine. His touch is warm, grounding, and when I meet his gaze, the red ring around his pupils seems to burn brighter, as if he’s holding back a firestorm of emotion.

“You deserved that moment,” he says softly, his voice low but firm. “You deserved to have your family back, to feel that love again.”

I swallow hard, nodding as the tears finally spill over. “I didn’t dare to dream of it,” I admit. “Not after everything.”

He squeezes my hand gently, his thumb brushing over my knuckles. "You've always deserved more than what this world gave you," he murmurs, his tone heavy with conviction. "And I will make sure you never have to live without it again."

His words settle over me, a promise as much as a vow, and for the first time in a long time, I feel a flicker of hope. Not just for the past, but for the future Rhadis and I are building together—one where I don't have to dream of love and safety anymore, because they're already within my grasp.

CHAPTER ELEVEN

As we finish eating, I set my fork down and lean back in my chair, letting out a small sigh of contentment. "The coffee was almost as good as the food," I remark, lifting the half-empty mug to my lips for one last sip.

Rhadis gives me a faint smirk, his dark eyes softening as he watches me. “Almost? I’ll have to let them know they’re slacking,” he says dryly, motioning to the waitress.

When she brings the bill, he pays without hesitation, sliding a few extra coins onto the table as a tip. “We should head back,” he says, rising from his chair and waiting for me to follow. His tone shifts as we step outside, the warmth of the diner replaced by the brisk bite of the winter air. “We need to discuss our plans.”

I nod, falling into step beside him as we walk down the quiet paths. “What are Ymir’s powers like?” I ask, glancing up at him.

He’s quiet for a moment, his expression darkening as he considers the question. “As the God of Revenge, his powers are fueled by anger,” he begins, his voice steady but low. “It’s not like any power you or I would use. It's… reactive, volatile. The more enraged he gets, the stronger he becomes."

I shiver slightly, not just from the cold but from the weight of his words. "How do you stop someone like that?" I ask quietly.

"That's the problem," Rhadis says, his jaw tightening. "I don't know how to stop him from getting worse while also keeping him away from the entrance to the underworld. And…" He hesitates, his tone dipping into something darker. "I've been told I can't fight him. Or kill him. That's not what the fates want."

The frustration in his voice is palpable, and I feel it echo in my own chest. "So what do we do?" I ask, stopping in my tracks to face him. "If we can't fight him, if you can't fight him, how do we keep him away?"

Rhadis turns to look at me, his expression unreadable. "I don't know yet," he admits, his voice quieter now. "But we have to figure it out."

I chew on my bottom lip, my mind racing. The weight of the problem presses down on me, but I refuse to let it crush me. "What if we throw him off his path?" I suggest, my voice gaining strength as the idea takes shape.

Rhadis raises a brow, his interest piqued. "How?"

"We circulate rumors," I say, my tone more confident now. "The village folk are so fond of gossip. If we spread the right story, one he can't resist, he'll hear it. He'll follow it."

He watches me for a moment, his sharp gaze narrowing thoughtfully. "You think it'll work?"

"I do," I say firmly. "It's not about fighting him—it's about keeping him distracted. If he's chasing a false lead, he won't be anywhere near the entrance. And if we plan it right, we can keep him running in circles for weeks."

Rhadis is silent for a long moment, his eyes scanning my face as though searching for any sign of doubt. When he finally speaks, there's a faint smile tugging at the corner of his mouth. "You're brilliant," he says simply.

I can't help the small blush that rises to my cheeks at the praise, but I push it aside. "It's just an idea," I say, brushing it off.

"It's more than that," he counters, his voice steady. "It's a way forward. And that's exactly what we need right now."

He steps closer, his hand brushing against mine briefly before he pulls back. "We'll need to move quickly," he says, his tone returning to its usual commanding steadiness. "If we're going to spread these rumors, we'll need to start in the surrounding villages."

I nod, determination settling over me like armor. "Then let's get started."

Rhadis watches me for another moment, something warm and unspoken passing between us, before he turns and starts walking. I follow close behind, my mind already racing with the details we'll need to put the plan in motion.

Rhadis walks ahead of me, his stride purposeful as his thoughts seem to pull him inward. The shadows that seep from his skin swirl lazily around his form, creating an almost hypnotic effect against the soft light filtering through the trees. I can see the tension in his shoulders, the way his hands flex occasionally, as if his thoughts are pressing on him, weighing him down.

And yet, as serious as his demeanor is, I can't stop my gaze from wandering. My eyes drift lower, catching on the way his pants hug him perfectly, and I can't help but admire how firm and... well, perfect his backside looks. I feel a flush creep up my cheeks, but I don't stop staring, even as my pace slows slightly to appreciate the view.

I don't realize he's stopped walking until I bump into his back. My hands instinctively reach out to steady myself as I gasp, startled. "Sorry," I say quickly, stepping back.

He turns to me, a knowing smirk already pulling at his lips. His gaze locks onto mine, and I feel my embarrassment grow as I see the amusement dancing in his eyes. "Distracted, were you?" he asks, his voice low and laced with humor.

"I wasn't—" I start to deny it, but the words catch in my throat as his smirk deepens.

He crosses his arms, leaning slightly toward me. "I could feel your gaze," he says, his tone teasing. "And I know exactly what had you so distracted."

Heat floods my cheeks, and I look away, trying to compose myself. "You're imagining things," I mutter, though I know the lie is weak at best.

He laughs, the sound rich and warm, and I can feel it vibrate through me. "I think we both know I'm not," he replies, clearly enjoying my discomfort. He straightens, glancing ahead before nodding toward the trees. "We're about to approach the next village. Have you thought about what we should circulate?"

Grateful for the change in topic, I nod quickly. "Yes," I say, taking a steadying breath. "We should spread a rumor about a silver-haired woman seen at the market, visiting the medical cabin. Someone overhearing her asking how soon she would give birth, and if the doctor could tell if the child would inherit her null gifts."

He tilts his head, considering my words. "A null would certainly raise concerns," he says thoughtfully. "Especially in a place like this, where fear of the unknown drives most conversations."

"That's the idea," I reply, feeling a flicker of pride at his approval. "If we frame it as the villagers' fear of having a null so close, the rumor will spread naturally. It won't need much encouragement."

He nods, his dark eyes sharpening as his thoughts seem to align with mine. "It's a smart angle," he admits. "Ymir won't be able to resist chasing that lead. He'll think it's her, without question."

"Exactly," I say, feeling more confident now. "It plants the seed of doubt, and the rest will grow on its own."

Rhadis's smirk returns, though this time it's softer, tinged with something that almost feels like pride. "You're getting better at this," he says, his voice carrying a quiet warmth that catches me off guard.

"Better at what?" I ask, raising a brow.

"At thinking strategically," he replies. "At understanding how to use fear and whispers to your advantage. It's… impressive."

I blink, startled by the compliment, but his expression is genuine. For a moment, the tension between us shifts, softens, and I find myself smiling despite the heat still lingering in my cheeks.

"Let's see if the people of Tuinen are as fond of gossip as we hope," he says, turning and continuing down the path. His tone is lighter now, though the shadows around him remain, swirling faintly as if echoing his thoughts.

I follow, my steps a little quicker this time, my mind racing with the possibilities of what we might achieve. As the trees begin to thin, revealing the outlines of small cabins in the distance, I feel a quiet determination settle in my chest. We can do this. We have to. For the realm, for the people, and for each other.

The village is a patchwork of small wooden cabins, their shutters painted in soft, cheerful colors that contrast with the somber expressions of the people we meet. Rhadis and I step into the first cabin, the scent of freshly baked bread wafting through the air. It's a bakery, the shelves lined with loaves and pastries, but the warmth of the space doesn't extend to the baker behind the counter. His wary eyes follow us as we enter, his hands tightening on the dough he's kneading.

Rhadis leans casually against the counter, his shadowy presence commanding attention even in the quiet cabin. "We overheard something concerning at the market," he says, his voice low and calm, as though sharing a piece of gossip instead of planting a seed of fear. "A silver-haired woman was seen at the medical cabin, asking about the child she's carrying."

The baker's hands still, his brows furrowing. "Silver-haired?" he repeats, his tone hesitant but laced with curiosity. "You don't mean… the woman from the prophecy?"

Rhadis exchanges a glance with me, and I nod, my expression serious. "That's what they said," I add softly. "She asked if the child would inherit her null gifts. They were worried—terrified, really—that such a thing could happen so close to the village."

The baker's face pales slightly, his gaze darting to the window as though expecting danger to walk through the door at any moment. "A null here?" he mutters, his voice tinged with disbelief. "I thought they were just a story. That they couldn't—"

"They're real," Rhadis cuts in smoothly, his voice carrying just enough weight to silence any doubt. "And if one of them is here, it's something you should take seriously."

We leave the bakery with the baker's worried muttering trailing behind us and move on to the next cabin. It's a tailor's shop this time, the walls lined with bolts of fabric in every color imaginable. The tailor, a middle-aged woman with streaks of gray in her blue hair, looks up from her work with a cautious smile that falters as we share the same story. Her hands tremble slightly as she folds a piece of fabric, her lips pressing into a thin line.

By the third cabin, the fear in the villagers' eyes is unmistakable. The blacksmith listens in silence as Rhadis speaks, his hammer still poised over the glowing red metal he's been shaping. When we finish, he sets the hammer down with a heavy sigh, wiping sweat from his brow. "We don't need that kind of trouble here," he says gruffly. "If she's a null, she could bring danger to all of us. Guards would come looking for her even if she steals no gifts."

"That's exactly why you should spread the word," Rhadis replies, his tone steady and reasonable. "The sooner people know, the safer everyone will be."

By the time we reach the last cabin—a small general store filled with jars of preserves and rows of simple tools—the rumor has already taken on a life of its own. The shopkeeper, a wiry man with sharp eyes, greets us with a question before we can even open our mouths. "You've heard about the null woman, haven't you?" he asks, his voice low as though speaking too loudly might summon her.

Rhadis raises a brow, feigning mild surprise. "I've heard whispers," he says. "What have you heard?"

The shopkeeper leans in, his expression grave. "She's staying nearby—at the medical cabin in the main market of Ulopia, they say. Asking questions about her child. If it's a null too..." He shakes his head, his hands fidgeting with the edge of his apron. "We don't need that kind of thing here. Nulls attract trouble, everyone knows that."

I exchange a glance with Rhadis, barely containing my satisfaction. The fear is palpable now, the villagers' imaginations doing more work than we ever could. The rumor is spreading like wildfire, twisting and growing with each retelling.

"You're right to be cautious," I say softly, my voice tinged with concern. "It's better to be prepared than caught off guard."

The shopkeeper nods fervently, his eyes darting to the window. "I'll tell the others to be on the lookout. If she's still here, we need to make sure she knows she's not welcome."

Rhadis and I leave the shop, stepping back into the crisp afternoon air. The village hums with quiet tension now, whispers passing from person to person as we walk through the streets. I glance at Rhadis, his expression unreadable, but there's a sharpness in his gaze that tells me he's pleased.

"It's working," I murmur, my voice barely audible over the wind.

He nods, his lips curving into a faint smirk. "Now we just have to hope Ymir hears it."

CHAPTER TWELVE

The air in the last village of Tuinen hums with unease. As Rhadis and I step through the muddy streets, the whispers are nearly deafening. People move quickly, their heads low, their conversations cutting off as we approach. It's clear that the rumors we've been spreading have taken root—and flourished far beyond what we ever expected.

The first shop we enter is a modest apothecary. Shelves are lined with dried herbs and glass jars filled with powders and potions. The smell of lavender and sage lingers in the air, but it does nothing to calm the shopkeeper's nerves. She wrings her hands as she talks to Rhadis, her voice low and trembling.

"They say she's just days away from giving birth," the shopkeeper whispers, glancing toward the door as though expecting someone to burst in at any moment. "Another null, born right next to Tuinen… It's bad luck. Worse than that, it's dangerous. Do you think the stories are true?"

Rhadis offers a noncommittal shrug, his expression grave. "Stories like these usually have a kernel of truth," he says evenly.

"And if they're true, you're right to be cautious. Nulls bring chaos, whether they mean to or not."

The woman shudders, clutching a bundle of sage to her chest like a talisman. "May the Gods help us all."

We leave the apothecary and make our way to the next shop, a small bakery bustling with people despite the growing tension in the village. Inside, the rumor has taken on an almost mythic quality. The customers chatter in hushed tones, their fear palpable.

"They say she's staying in a cabin at the edge of Ulopia," a man murmurs to his wife as they pick up a loaf of bread. "The guards are already on their way. Can you imagine what would happen if she moves and is found here?"

"The whole village would be torn apart," the woman replies, clutching the bread like it's the last thing keeping her grounded. "We've already lost too much to the curse. We can't afford to lose anything else."

Rhadis steps closer, pretending to examine a row of pastries, and adds just enough fuel to their fire. "If the guards are involved, they'll search everywhere," he says lightly, his voice carrying just enough weight to make them listen. "I'd keep my distance from anyone suspicious. Just to be safe."

The couple nods quickly, exchanging worried glances before hurrying out of the bakery. I watch them go, a pang of guilt stirring in my chest, but I push it down. This is for the greater good. If Ymir follows these threads, it'll buy us the time we need.

By the time we reach the last cabin—a general store on the outskirts of the village—the rumor has snowballed into something far more dangerous. The shopkeeper, a wiry old man with a nervous twitch, greets us with wide eyes.

"You've heard, haven't you?" he asks before we can even speak, his voice a frantic whisper. "There's a God heading to Ulopia now. They say he's going to find her, the silver-haired woman, and deal with her before she brings ruin to the villages."

Rhadis stiffens beside me, his expression carefully neutral, but I feel the tension radiating off him. "A God?" he echoes, his voice low and measured. "Which one?"

The shopkeeper shakes his head, his hands fluttering like anxious birds. "I don't know. One of the Gods of Arrakis, I think. Someone powerful enough to put an end to it before it spreads any further. They said he shakes with fury as he speaks, that his anger grows by the minute and can be felt in the air. Thank the heavens for that."

I glance at Rhadis, catching the flicker of something dangerous in his eyes. He nods to the shopkeeper, muttering a polite thanks before steering me out of the cabin. As soon as the door closes behind us, his expression darkens.

"A God heading to Ulopia," he says under his breath, his voice tight with restrained anger. "The growing anger complicates things."

I wrap my arms around myself, the chill in the air biting through my coat. "Do you think it's Ymir?"

"Who else could it be?" Rhadis replies, his shadows seeping from his skin as he paces. "If he believes she's there, he won't stop until he finds her. And if the village is destroyed in the process..." He trails off, shaking his head. "We need to move. Now."

I nod, my heart pounding. The rumors have done their job—perhaps too well. But as fear grips the villages and Ymir closes in on Ulopia, I can't help but wonder if we've set something in motion that we can't control.

Rhadis moves with practiced efficiency, his shadows swirling as he changes the small cabin back into the tent it once was. The dark energy seems to seep into the wood and stone, pulling it apart and reshaping it into fabric, poles, and ropes. I watch, fascinated and a little unsettled by how seamlessly his power bends the physical world to his will.

"Pack the furs," he says without looking at me, his voice firm but calm. "We'll need them in Ulopia."

I nod, gathering the soft furs and folding them into a neat bundle. The cool winter air nips at my skin, and I find myself grateful for the coat he made me wear earlier. Despite the rush, Rhadis seems steady, his movements deliberate as he rolls up the tent and ties it securely to his pack.

When he finishes, he slings the pack over his shoulder and turns to me. "We're heading to the main market within Ulopia," he says, his dark eyes meeting mine. "It's a harsh land but this village is the easiest for survival so it is heavily populated—crowded enough to keep us hidden, but close enough to the villages that we'll hear anything about Ymir's movements."

I nod again, trusting his judgment even as a twinge of unease settles in my chest. "And if he follows the rumors to the villages?"

Rhadis's lips press into a thin line, the faint red rings around his pupils glowing slightly. "Then we protect the people and keep him away from the gifted living there. No one else needs to suffer because of him."

He steps closer, his hand brushing lightly against mine. "Are you ready?"

I take a deep breath and nod. "Yes."

He places his hand on my shoulder, and the world shifts. The familiar tingling sensation of his magic spreads through me, wrapping around my body like a warm, heavy fur. The ground beneath my feet disappears, replaced by a swirling darkness that feels both endless and comforting. For a moment, there's nothing but the sensation of movement, like being carried on a current I can't see.

When I open my eyes, we're standing outside a circle of wooden cabins. The air here is warmer, the breeze carrying the scent of spices and baked goods. The only entrance to the circle is a massive stone arch nestled between two of the cabins, its surface etched with intricate carvings that seem to shimmer faintly in the sunlight.

"This is Ulopia," Rhadis says, his voice steady as he surveys the area. "The market is just beyond that arch. It's one of the busiest trade hubs in the realm."

I take in the sight before me, the bustling energy of the village already palpable even from outside the arch. People move in and out of the stone circle, their arms laden with baskets and bundles, their voices carrying snippets of conversation and laughter. The gifted here are varied in color of skin, hair and gifts. Despite the warmth and activity, I can't shake the feeling that we're being watched, that danger is closer than it seems.

Rhadis leads me through the arch and into the heart of the village. The streets are lined with colorful stalls and small shops, their displays bursting with goods—silks, spices, jewelry, and more. The air is thick with the mingling scents of fresh bread, roasted meats, and sweet honey cakes. It's almost overwhelming, but there's a strange sense of comfort in the chaos.

"We'll stay here," Rhadis says, guiding me toward a modest inn on the edge of the market square. Its wooden sign swings gently in the breeze, the faded lettering reading **The Traveler's Hearth.**

Inside, the Inn is warm and inviting, with low wooden beams and a roaring fire in the hearth. The innkeeper, a plump woman with kind eyes, greets us with a smile that fades slightly as her gaze lingers on Rhadis. I wonder if she senses his power, the darkness that always seems to follow him, but she says nothing and hands us a key with only a slight tremor in her hand.

"Our room is on the second floor," Rhadis says, his voice low as he leads me up the creaking stairs. "We'll use this as our base for now. From here, we can monitor the market and keep an ear out for any news about Ymir."

The room is small but clean, with a single cot pushed against one wall and a narrow window overlooking the market below. I set the furs on the cot and turn to Rhadis, who's already surveying the room with a critical eye.

"It'll do," he says finally, setting his pack down by the door. He turns to me, his expression softening slightly. "Get some rest if you need it. We'll need to be alert once the market opens fully."

I nod, though I know rest will be the last thing on my mind. As Rhadis moves to unpack, I glance out the window, watching the vibrant life of Ulopia unfold below. The people here seem happy, unaware of the danger that lurks just beyond their village. I can only hope that we're in time to keep it that way.

Rhadis looks up from unpacking, his dark eyes softening as they meet mine. "You want to visit the market don't you?" he asks, a small smile tugging at the corner of his mouth.

I nod, my excitement barely contained. "I've never been to one before. I'd love to see it."

He chuckles, shaking his head slightly as he sets the last of our things down. "Of course, we can go," he says, crossing the small room to stand in front of me. He reaches out, pulling me into his arms with an ease that still catches me off guard. The strength in his hold is steady, grounding, and when he presses a kiss to the top of my head, I feel a warmth bloom in my chest.

"Let's go, then," he murmurs, his voice low and affectionate. "Before you start listing all the reasons why we should have gone sooner."

I laugh softly, letting him guide me out of the inn and into the bustling village. The market is alive with color and sound, every corner filled with energy that seems to hum in the air. Stalls line the streets, their displays bursting with goods—vibrant fabrics, glittering jewelry, and baskets overflowing with fresh produce. The scent of roasted meats and sweet pastries wafts through the air, mingling with the chatter of merchants and customers.

Rhadis's hand finds mine as we weave through the crowd, his grip firm and reassuring. "What would you like to see first?" he asks, his voice calm despite the chaos around us.

I glance around, taking in the sheer variety of sights and sounds, before my gaze lands on a small platform at the edge of the square. Six people stand there, their hands moving expertly over harps as they sing in perfect harmony. "The music," I say, smiling up at him. "I'd like to listen to the music."

He nods, his lips quirking into a faint smile, and leads me toward the platform. The crowd thins slightly as we reach the edge, and I find myself captivated by the hauntingly beautiful melody that fills the air. The musicians' voices blend seamlessly, their song weaving a tale of a God fighting to protect his lands.

I squeeze Rhadis's hand gently, glancing up at him. "Does it feel strange to hear them sing about the Gods?" I ask softly. "Since... well, since you are one?"

He shakes his head, his expression thoughtful. "No," he says simply. "It's all I've ever known. The stories, the songs—they've always been there. They don't phase me."

The song shifts then, the melody growing darker, more chilling. The musicians' voices drop to a lower tone as they sing of a God sent to the Underworld, his journey through a realm filled with danger and despair. The lyrics are vivid, painting a picture of shadowy landscapes and treacherous trials.

I glance at Rhadis, his expression unreadable as he listens. But then he chuckles softly, the sound warm and reassuring. "Even when I visited as a child," he says, his voice quiet but steady, "I knew the realm was mine. It held no danger for me."

The calm confidence in his tone sends a shiver through me—not of fear, but of awe. "You weren't afraid?" I ask, my voice barely above a whisper.

He shakes his head, his gaze distant as if he's recalling the memories. "No. The Underworld has always been… familiar. It's a part of me, just as much as I'm a part of it."

I look back at the musicians, their song still echoing through the square, and for a moment, I try to imagine what it must have been like for him—to grow up knowing he belonged to a place so feared by others. The thought fills me with a quiet sense of wonder, and as I glance back at him, I can't help but feel a deeper appreciation for the man beside me.

The music swells, the voices rising in a haunting crescendo, and I squeeze his hand again, grounding myself in the warmth of his presence. Whatever the stories say, whatever fears the world might hold, I know that with Rhadis, I am safe.

Rhadis holds me close as the music changes once again, his hand firm on my lower back. The haunting melodies have shifted into something more uplifting, the notes carrying hope and resilience. I relax into him, letting myself enjoy the moment of peace in the vibrant marketplace. His body is warm and steady, a solid presence that feels like home, no matter where we are.

After the second song finishes, I step back, looking up at him with a small smile. "I think I've heard enough music for now," I say softly. "I'd like to visit some shops."

He arches a brow, a playful smirk tugging at the corner of his lips. "Shops, huh? Any particular kind, or are we just browsing?"

"Browsing," I reply, a hint of excitement in my voice. "I want to see what they have here."

He nods, his smirk softening into a genuine smile, and he takes my hand, leading me toward a row of shops lining one of the quieter streets. The first one we enter is a bedding store, its walls lined with plush accent pieces, pillows, and furs in every color and texture imaginable.

I run my fingers over a thick white fur draped over a display cot, marveling at its softness. "This is incredible," I murmur, brushing my hand over it again. "How do people even travel with cots this big? How do they get them to their homes?"

Rhadis chuckles, his deep voice reverberating in the cozy shop. "They don't, not usually. The shops here offer shipping carriages for larger purchases. You buy something like this,"—he gestures to an oversized cot piled high with pillows and furs—"and they'll deliver it directly to your home."

I glance at him, my brows raising in curiosity. "Shipping carriages? Like entire wagons just for deliveries?"

He nods, leaning casually against one of the wooden support beams. "Exactly. They've got whole systems in place for it—teams of horses, mapped-out routes, the works. It's a decent business, especially in places like this where people travel light due to the land's hostility but want to furnish their homes with quality goods."

I turn back to the display, running my fingers over a set of silky pillows embroidered with intricate patterns. "That's fascinating. I never thought about how people manage to get things like this back to their homes."

His gaze softens as he watches me, his arms crossing over his chest. "You don't realize how rare it is to see someone so genuinely curious about the world, do you?" he says quietly, almost to himself.

I glance back at him, tilting my head. "What do you mean?"

He pushes off the beam and steps closer, his fingers brushing against mine as I linger over the pillows. "I mean," he says, his voice low, "you don't take anything for granted. Even the simplest things—you want to know how they work, why they're there. It's… refreshing."

I feel heat rise to my cheeks at his words, and I duck my head, focusing on the pillow beneath my hand. "Well, I guess I just… never had the chance to wonder about these things before. Everything feels so new to me now."

He nods, his hand settling lightly on my back. "Then let's see more," he says with a small smile. "Whatever catches your eye."

I return his smile, letting him guide me toward another part of the shop, eager to explore everything this place has to offer.

The cabin labeled **Mates** catches my eye, its sign hanging delicately from a post with intricate carvings of vines and flowers. I tug Rhadis's hand gently. "Can we stop here?"

He glances at the sign, his expression unreadable for a moment, then nods. "Absolutely, my mate."

The small cabin smells of lavender and something warm, like fresh parchment and soft earth. Inside, strips of long fabric in every shade imaginable drape the walls, their textures and colors captivating. I run my fingers over one, a deep green that reminds me of the shade Rhadis seems to favor. The fabric is soft and light, like a whisper beneath my touch.

I turn, noticing a stand of rings glinting in the soft light near the corner. "Come look at these," I say, pulling him toward it.

He follows, his towering frame casting a shadow over the delicate display. The rings are breathtaking—each one unique, with intricate metalwork and stones that seem to shimmer with their own light. Some are simple bands, elegant in their minimalism, while others are adorned with small carvings, braided patterns, or swirling designs etched into the metal. The stones range from deep greens and blues to fiery reds and soft opals that catch the light beautifully.

As I pick up a ring with a small moonstone set into a silver band,

I glance up at him and catch him smiling down at me. "What?" I ask, tilting my head.

He shakes his head slightly, his smile widening. "Nothing. Just... watching you."

I narrow my eyes playfully. "What are you thinking?"

He hesitates for a moment, his gaze flicking briefly to the rings before returning to mine. "This cabin," he says softly, "is for mating ceremonies. These fabrics, these rings... they're for completing the bond that ties two mates together. Not just in this life, but in every life after."

His words settle over me like a warm breeze, stirring something deep in my chest. I look back down at the ring in my hand, tracing the smooth stone with my thumb. "So, this is where people come to... seal their bond?" I ask, my voice quieter now.

"Yes," he says, his voice low, almost reverent. "It's a promise. A vow."

I look back up at him, my heart fluttering. "Can we have a ceremony?"

Before he can answer, a soft voice speaks from behind us. "You can."

I whirl around, startled, to see a man stepping out from a small door at the back of the cabin. He's tall and thin, his white robes brushing the wooden floor as he approaches. His eyes glint with an otherworldly light, his presence commanding but gentle, as if he's part of the fabric of the cabin itself.

"I can feel the fates woven between you," he says, his voice rich and soothing. "Yours is a bond already strong, but if you wish to solidify it, I can perform the ceremony."

I glance at Rhadis, my breath catching as I search his face. His dark eyes are thoughtful, the red ring around his pupils faint but steady, and then he nods slowly.

"If this is what you want," he says softly, "then yes. Let's complete our bond."

The warmth in his voice makes my heart swell, and I turn back to the man, my voice steady with excitement. "I want this. I want us to be fully bonded."

The man smiles, the corners of his eyes crinkling. "Then let us begin."

The man leads us to the center of the cabin, where a small altar is draped in soft, woven fabric. The lavender scent grows stronger as he picks up a bundle of green strips from the table. The fabric gleams faintly, as if enchanted, and he lays it across his palms with care.

"This ceremony," he begins, his voice calm and steady, "is not just for your bond in this life, but for every life that comes after. The fates have already chosen you for each other. What we do here today acknowledges and strengthens that connection."

Rhadis's hand brushes mine, and I glance at him. His dark eyes are steady, a rare softness in his expression. The faint red glow around his pupils is almost soothing, a reminder of his power and presence, but right now, it feels like he's entirely mine.

"Stand facing one another," the rabbi instructs, gesturing for us to move closer.

I turn to Rhadis, my breath catching at how tall and steady he looks. His hands are scarred, his shoulders broad and strong, and yet his expression is tender as he reaches for me. He takes my hands in his, his touch warm and grounding, and for a moment, the rest of the world seems to fall away.

The rabbi takes one of the green bands and wraps it around our joined hands, weaving it slowly between our fingers. The fabric is impossibly soft, almost weightless, but the moment it touches my skin, I feel a quiet hum of energy, like the fabric itself is alive.

"This band," the rabbi says, "represents the threads of your lives, woven together by the fates. It is not a bond of ownership or control, but one of partnership and trust."

He loops the band again, this time tying it loosely around our wrists so that neither of us can let go without untying it. The knot rests between our palms, and I feel the warmth of Rhadis's skin through the fabric.

"You may now speak your vows," the rabbi says, stepping back slightly to give us space.

Rhadis's grip on my hands tightens slightly, and he looks at me with an intensity that makes my breath hitch. "Raya," he begins, his voice low but steady, "from the moment we were children, I knew you were special. You challenged me, grounded me, and even in your defiance, you made me better. I've waited for this—for you—for longer than I can say. I vow to protect you, to honor you, and to stand beside you in every life. You are my equal, my partner, and my reason."

His words send a warmth flooding through me, my chest tightening with emotion. I blink quickly, willing away the tears that threaten to fall, and take a shaky breath. "Rhadis," I begin, my voice trembling but resolute, "I've spent so much of my life trying to survive, trying to find a place where I belonged. With you, I've found that place. You've seen me at my worst, and still, you've given me nothing but strength and love. I vow to stand with you, to be your partner, your equal, in this life and all the ones to come. You are my home."

The rabbi smiles faintly, his gaze warm and approving. He takes another band, this one a darker shade of green, and ties it over the first, the layers of fabric binding us closer.

The rabbi steps back after tying the last band, lifting his hands toward the ceiling as if addressing something higher than any of us. His voice is rich and resonant, filling the small cabin with a quiet reverence.

"We thank the gods and the fates," he intones, his gaze drifting upward, "for weaving this union into the tapestry of existence. By their design, your souls have been bound through lifetimes, and today you affirm that bond with your hearts and your choices."

I glance at Rhadis, feeling the weight of the moment settle over us. His eyes are locked on mine, the red rings around his pupils glowing faintly, his expression unwavering. I squeeze his hand lightly, grounding myself in his steady presence.

The rabbi reaches into a small, ornate box on the altar and removes two rings, holding them out for us to take. Each is unique, the metal gleaming softly in the cabin's dim light. The one meant for Rhadis is simple, a dark band with faint, swirling etchings that remind me of the shadows that seep from his skin. The other is for me—a delicate band of ashy green metal, almost silver in certain lights, with a single, smooth stone embedded in its center. The stone catches the light in subtle, shifting hues, like a forest at dusk.

"These rings," the rabbi says, his voice filled with quiet power, "are symbols of your union, a physical reminder of the bond you have chosen to embrace. Place them on one another's hands, so that the realms may see and know your connection."

Rhadis takes my ring first, holding it carefully between his fingers. He lifts my left hand, his touch warm and sure, and slides the band onto my finger. The metal feels cool at first, but as it settles into place, a quiet hum of energy pulses through me, as though the ring itself acknowledges its purpose.

"You're mine," he murmurs softly, his voice low enough that only I can hear. There's no arrogance in the words, only a quiet reverence that sends warmth flooding through my chest.

I take his ring next, my hands trembling slightly as I lift it. My fingers brush against his as I guide the band onto his hand, the dark metal contrasting lightly with his dark skin. It suits him perfectly—strong, understated, and undeniably him.

"And you're mine," I say quietly, my voice steady despite the rush of emotion building inside me.

The rabbi steps back, his smile soft but filled with quiet authority. "By the Gods' will and the fates' design, you are now bound in heart, in soul, and in death. You have affirmed your connection and chosen each other, not just for this life, but for all that follow."

He pauses, his gaze sweeping over us both, and when he speaks again, his voice is softer, almost intimate. "You are now free to complete the bond in body as you have in soul. Go forward together, with the blessings of the Gods and the strength of your union."

The weight of his words lingers in the air, and I feel my breath catch as I look at Rhadis. His eyes burn with a quiet intensity, the red rings glowing faintly as his lips curve into a small, knowing smile. He lifts my hand to his lips, brushing a kiss over my newly adorned ring finger, and the simple gesture makes my heart flutter.

The rabbi steps aside, his presence fading into the background as if to give us space. Rhadis turns to me fully, his hand still holding mine, and for a moment, it feels like the world has narrowed to just the two of us.

"You're mine, Raya," he says again, his voice low and filled with a quiet certainty. "In every way that matters."

"And you're mine," I reply, my voice soft but resolute. The ashy green stone on my finger glints faintly in the light, a quiet promise of what we've chosen.

We unwrap the fabric and leave the cabin together, making our way through the market. As we step into the inn, the warm scent of wood and faint herbs fills the air, but I barely notice it. My attention is drawn to my arm as I catch a glint of light. There, within the dark mark of our original mating band, is a small, faint gold line, delicate and shimmering. It wasn't there before. My fingers brush over it, the metallic gleam catching the light, and I smile, my chest filling with a quiet warmth.

I glance at Rhadis, and my smile widens when I see the same golden band etched into the mark on his arm. It's subtle, but it's there, a sign of what we've just promised each other, what we've made permanent.

He notices my gaze and follows it to his own arm, a small smirk tugging at his lips. "The fates have their way of making things known," he says softly, his tone warm but teasing. "As if we needed another reminder of what we are to each other."

I laugh lightly, the sound carrying a mix of relief and joy. "I think it's perfect," I say, still tracing the golden band with my fingertips. "It feels... complete now."

Rhadis watches me for a moment, his expression softening in a way that he rarely lets anyone else see. Then, without a word, he reaches for my hand and pulls me gently toward him. His touch is warm, grounding, as he leads me further into the room. The door closes quietly behind us, and the world outside seems to fade away.

Once we're alone, he turns to me, his gaze steady and filled with an intensity that makes my heart race. "Raya," he murmurs, his voice low, and the way he says my name sends a shiver down my spine.

Before I can respond, he steps closer, his hands finding my waist as he pulls me against him. His touch is firm but gentle, his presence as steady as ever, and when he leans down, his lips brush mine in a kiss so soft it feels like a whisper.

The warmth of him surrounds me, his scent—dark and earthy—filling the space between us. The kiss deepens gradually, his hands sliding up my back, pulling me closer still. I melt into him, my hands finding their way to his chest, feeling the steady thrum of his heartbeat beneath my fingertips.

When he pulls back, his forehead rests against mine, his breath mingling with mine in the quiet of the room. "You're mine now," he says softly, the words not a claim but a quiet promise. His eyes meet mine, the red ring around his pupils glowing faintly, a reminder of what we've just shared.

"And you're mine," I reply, my voice barely above a whisper. The golden band on my arm seems to pulse faintly, as though it's alive, mirroring the rhythm of my heartbeat.

For a moment, we simply stand there, holding each other, the weight of the day settling into a quiet, shared peace. The world outside is distant, its troubles kept at bay, and all that matters is this—this moment, this connection, this bond that feels unbreakable.

Rhadis steps back slightly, his hands still resting lightly on my hips. His dark eyes search mine, the faint red rings glowing with an intensity that makes my breath hitch.

"Are you ready?" he asks, his voice low and steady, laced with something deeper—anticipation, reverence, and a quiet, simmering heat.

I nod, my voice soft but certain. "Yes."

His lips curve into a slow, deliberate smile, and his hands move to the ties of my dress. His touch is gentle but deliberate, the movements unhurried as he untangles the knots and loosens the fabric. The dress slides from my shoulders, pooling at my feet in a soft whisper, leaving me bare before him.

The cool air of the room brushes against my skin, but the warmth of his gaze is enough to banish any chill. His eyes roam over me, dark and unrelenting, and the low groan that escapes his lips sends a shiver through my body.

I shift nervously, unsure what to do under his scrutiny, but the sound of his voice steadies me. "Raya," he murmurs, his tone rough and filled with something I can't quite name. "You're more beautiful than anything I have ever seen."

The words make my cheeks flush, but before I can respond, a quiet giggle escapes me. The sound surprises me, light and unexpected, and it only grows louder when I see the way his eyes widen slightly at the movement of my chest. My giggle makes my breasts bounce subtly, and his deep groan this time is louder, more guttural.

"You're going to drive me mad," he says, his voice tight with restraint.

I can't help but laugh again, though the sound is softer this time, more intimate. “I thought I already had,” I tease, and his lips twitch into a smirk, though his eyes stay locked on me.

“Turn for me,” he says, his tone deepening, thick with want. “I want to see all of you, my mate.”

The way he says “my mate” sends heat coursing through me, pooling low in my belly. I hesitate for only a moment before nodding and stepping back slightly. Slowly, I turn, my movements deliberate, feeling the weight of his gaze as it traces every inch of my skin.

His breath hitches as I complete the circle, my back to him now, and I feel the heat of his hand ghosting over my lower back. He doesn’t touch me, not yet, but the warmth of his presence is enough to set my nerves alight.

“You’re perfect,” he murmurs, his voice barely above a whisper, as though the words are meant for him alone. His hand finally comes to rest on my hip, his thumb brushing over my skin in a soothing, deliberate motion. “Every inch of you.”

His words make my chest tighten, a mix of vulnerability and warmth flooding me as I turn to face him again. His eyes meet mine, and the intensity there takes my breath away. It’s not just desire I see—it’s devotion, a quiet promise that I know will last far longer than this moment.

“Come here,” he says, his voice softer now, and his arms open slightly in invitation.

I step forward, into his warmth, and his hands find their way to my waist again, pulling me closer. The heat of his skin against mine is electrifying, grounding me and overwhelming me all at once. When he leans down to press his lips to mine, I melt into him, the world around us fading until there's nothing left but him.

As I tug at the ties of his pants, my fingers tremble slightly, anticipation making my heart race. His lips never leave mine, our kisses deepening with each passing moment. His hands move to my waist, steadying me as I work, the fabric slipping loose and falling away. His warm, bare skin brushes against me, and I let out a soft gasp when I feel the heat of his body press closer.

Between kisses, Rhadis pulls his shirt over his head in one smooth motion, and the sight of him—completely bare—steals my breath. The broad expanse of his chest, the scars that map the story of his life, the power in every line of his body—it's all consuming. My hands instinctively reach for him, running along his shoulders and down his arms as he steps closer, pulling me against him.

He breaks the kiss for a moment, his eyes locking onto mine, glowing faintly in the dim light of the room. "You're stunning, Raya," he murmurs, his voice low and reverent, the words a quiet promise.

Before I can respond, his lips find mine again, more insistent now, his dominance clear as he guides me backward toward the cot. The soft furs brush against the backs of my legs, and he lowers me onto them with care, his hands never leaving my body.

I sink into the softness beneath me, my breathing uneven as his kisses trail from my lips to my jaw, then down to the sensitive curve of my neck. His hands move with purpose, grazing over my sides, my waist, my thighs, leaving a trail of fire in their wake.

"Rhadis," I whisper, his name a breathless plea on my lips as his kisses grow more fervent, more consuming.

He shifts slightly, settling over me, his strong frame surrounding me in warmth and power. One hand tangles in my hair, tilting my head back as his lips capture mine again. This kiss is different—deeper, hungrier. It's not just a kiss; it's a claim, a declaration of everything he feels but hasn't yet put into words.

His other hand explores my body, grazing over my ribs before brushing over the curve of my breast. The sensation makes me arch into him, a soft moan escaping before I can stop it. He groans in response, the sound vibrating against my lips as his hand continues its journey, teasing and caressing with a confidence that leaves me trembling beneath him.

"You're mine," he murmurs against my skin, his voice rough with emotion as his lips trail lower, leaving a path of heat and longing in their wake. "Every inch of you, Raya. Mine."

The words send a shiver through me, the intensity of his gaze and touch overwhelming in the best way. I reach for him, my hands running over the hard planes of his back, desperate to feel closer, to give as much as I take. Every kiss, every touch, every whispered word binds us closer together, a perfect storm of passion and devotion.

Rhadis's lips leave a trail of warmth and fire as they move lower, his kisses slow and deliberate. My breathing hitches when he pauses at my breasts, his mouth closing over one nipple as his hand gently teases the other. The sensation sends a wave of pleasure through me, my back arching instinctively as a soft moan escapes my lips.

He chuckles against my skin, the vibration sending sparks racing through my body. "So responsive," he murmurs, his voice thick with admiration and something darker, hungrier. "Every sound you make drives me mad."

His kisses trail lower, over my stomach, the heat of his mouth lingering with every touch. My fingers tangle in the furs beneath me, my chest rising and falling with shallow breaths as I try to steady myself. But when his hands part my thighs, his lips brushing softly against the sensitive skin there, all thoughts scatter.

He settles between my legs, his broad shoulders framing me as he looks up, his glowing eyes locking onto mine. His gaze is intense, filled with a mix of adoration and determination that sends a new wave of heat flooding through me.

"Raya," he says softly, his voice low and commanding all at once. "I'm going to make you cum. I'm going to get you ready for me."

The promise in his words makes my heart race, anticipation and vulnerability blending into something electrifying. I can only nod, my voice lost to the whirlwind of emotions coursing through me.

His lips press against me, soft at first, testing, tasting. The sensation is like nothing I've ever felt, my entire body jolting with the intensity of it. He starts slowly, his tongue tracing gentle patterns, and I can't stop the quiet gasp that escapes me.

"You're already so wet for me," he murmurs against my skin, his voice rough with need. "So perfect."

The sound of his voice, the heat of his mouth—it's all too much and not enough. My hands find their way to his hair, threading through the soft strands as he continues. His tongue moves with precision, each stroke building the pressure in my core, winding it tighter and tighter until I feel like I might shatter.

"Rhadis," I whisper, his name a plea as my hips shift against him, chasing the relief I can feel hovering just out of reach.

He groans in response, his hands gripping my thighs to hold me in place as he deepens his movements, his tongue finding a rhythm that leaves me trembling. One hand slips up, his fingers brushing over my entrance, teasing, before one slides inside me. The combination of his mouth and his touch steals my breath, my body arching off the cot as the tension in my core builds to an unbearable peak.

"That little gasp you make right there. Gods, it drives me insane," he murmurs, his voice dark and full of reverence. "You're so response. So sensitive. Like you know exactly how to fall apart for me."

His words send me over the edge, the pressure bursting into a wave of pleasure that crashes through me. My body shakes, my fingers tightening in his hair as I cry out, my release rolling through me in waves that leave me breathless.

Rhadis doesn't stop, his movements slowing but never ceasing as he guides me through the aftershocks, his hands steadying me as my body trembles beneath him. When I finally catch my breath, my head falls back against the furs, my chest rising and falling with the effort of it.

He kisses his way back up my body, his lips soft and lingering, and when he reaches my face, he presses a gentle kiss to my forehead. "You're perfect, Raya," he whispers, his voice filled with a tenderness that makes my chest ache. "Absolutely perfect."

I look up at him, my heart still racing, and I can't help the smile that spreads across my lips. "That was... incredible," I manage, my voice still shaky.

He grins, his expression softening as he brushes a strand of hair from my face. "And I'm not done yet." His voice carries a promise that sends a shiver down my spine, the heat in his gaze reigniting as he leans down to kiss me again, deeper this time, his body pressing against mine.

Rhadis cradles me against him, his lips never straying far from mine. His body is warm, his skin firm under my touch, and every kiss he gives me feels like a promise. But then I feel it—him, the tip of him pressing against my core. My body tenses with anticipation, and a shiver of heat ripples through me, igniting something deep inside.

He pauses, his eyes meeting mine. They're dark, intense, the red ring glowing and swirling. "Raya," he whispers, his voice low and reverent, "are you sure?"

My breath catches, but I don't hesitate. "I want to feel you," I murmur, my voice barely more than a whisper. "I want you inside me."

The groan that escapes him is primal, deep, and it sends a thrill coursing through me. His hands glide down my body, steadying me as his lips capture mine again, the kiss filled with both hunger and tenderness. Slowly, deliberately, he adjusts his hips, his body pressing closer to mine.

The moment he starts to push inside me, I gasp. The sensation is overwhelming—a mix of fullness, heat, and a delicious stretch that steals my breath. He moves slowly, his hands steady on my hips as he gives me time to adjust, his lips brushing against mine in soft, grounding kisses.

"You're so tight," he murmurs, his voice rough, almost strained. "So perfect."

I shiver at his words, my hands clutching at his shoulders as he presses further, filling me inch by inch. The heat building in my core intensifies, my body trembling under the weight of it. Every movement feels deliberate, as though he's savoring every second, every reaction I give him.

When he's fully seated inside me, he stills, his forehead pressing against mine. Both of us are breathing hard, the moment heavy with emotion and connection. "Raya," he murmurs, his voice full of wonder, "you feel... incredible."

"So do you," I manage, my voice trembling but sincere. The sensation of him inside me is unlike anything I've ever felt—intimate, overwhelming, and deeply right.

He kisses me again, slow and deep, as his hips begin to move. The rhythm is gentle at first, his movements careful as he gauges my reactions. But as my body relaxes, as I start to meet his thrusts with my own, his pace quickens, the intensity building between us.

Every stroke sends a new wave of pleasure crashing through me, the friction and heat pulling soft moans from my lips. His hands are everywhere—my hips, my waist, my thighs—his touch grounding me even as I feel like I'm unraveling under him.

"You feel so perfect wrapped around me," he whispers, his voice rough with need. "I could stay like this forever, watching you, feeling you, worshipping you."

His words push me closer to the edge, the coil in my core tightening with every thrust. I cling to him, my nails digging into his shoulders as I lose myself in the rhythm, in the way our bodies move together as if they were made for this.

"Rhadis," I breathe, his name a plea on my lips as the pressure builds to an unbearable peak.

"I've got you," he murmurs, his lips brushing against my ear as he thrusts deeper, his movements growing more powerful, more insistent. "Let go, Raya. I'm here."

And with that, I shatter, the pleasure crashing over me in waves so intense I can't hold back the cry that escapes my lips.

My body tightens around him, and he groans, his own release following shortly after. He holds me tightly as he spills inside me, his movements slowing but never stopping, riding out the aftershocks of pleasure together.

When we finally still, both of us breathing hard, he presses a soft kiss to my forehead, his hands stroking my hair as he holds me close. “You’re everything to me,” he whispers, his voice soft but full of conviction. “My mate, my world.”

I smile, my heart full as I nestle closer to him, feeling the warmth of his body and the steady beat of his heart against mine. “And you’re mine,” I whisper back, the truth of it settling over me like a warm embrace.

CHAPTER THIRTEEN

The soft light of morning filters into the room, casting a golden glow over the walls. I stir awake, the haze of sleep still clinging to me, but something warm and familiar pulls me fully into consciousness. A gasp escapes my lips as I realize what it is—Rhadis, his head nestled between my thighs, his tongue working me with slow, deliberate strokes.

"Rhadis," I murmur, my voice breathy and still heavy with sleep. My hands instinctively reach down, curling in his dark hair, tugging gently as pleasure ripples through me.

He hums against me, the vibration sending a fresh wave of heat coursing through my core. His hands grip my thighs, holding me in place as he alternates between flicking his tongue against the sensitive bundle of nerves and delving deeper, tasting me like I'm the finest meal he's ever had.

"You're awake," he murmurs, pulling back just enough to smirk up at me, the faint red ring around his pupils glowing softly in the morning light. "Good. I didn't want you to miss this."

I can't help but laugh, though it's shaky and cut off by a sharp intake of breath as his fingers join in. One slides inside me, then another, his touch both careful and commanding. He moves with a practiced rhythm, curling his fingers just right, coaxing moans from my lips that I can't hold back.

The sensations build quickly, my body responding to him in ways I never thought possible. My hips lift off the cot, seeking more, chasing the release I know only he can give me. "Rhadis," I gasp again, his name a plea, a prayer, a tether keeping me grounded as the pressure coils tighter and tighter inside me.

"Let go, Raya," he whispers against my skin, his voice low and rough with desire. "I've got you. Always."

And I do. My body trembles, pleasure crashing over me in waves so powerful I forget to breathe for a moment. My hands clutch at the furs beneath me, my head tilting back as I cry out, his name spilling from my lips like a mantra.

He doesn't stop, his movements slowing only when I'm completely spent, my body limp and trembling beneath him. He kisses the inside of my thigh, soft and reverent, before sitting up and meeting my gaze, a smug grin tugging at his lips.

"Now that I've had my breakfast," he says, his voice light and teasing, though his eyes are still dark with satisfaction, "it's time to take you into the village and feed you."

A breathless laugh escapes me, and I reach out to smack his shoulder playfully. "You're batty," I say, though I can't help but smile.

"And yet, you're mine," he replies, leaning down to steal a quick kiss before helping me sit up. His touch is gentle, his hands steadying me as I try to gather myself. "Come on, mate. Let's see what trouble we can find in the village today."

As I dress and he watches with that same satisfied smirk, I can't help but feel the warmth in my chest spread. It's not just the afterglow of what just happened; it's the comfort of knowing I'm with him, and with him, I'll always be safe, cherished, and, apparently, very well-fed.

As we walk toward the diner, the morning air is crisp, carrying the faint scent of blooming flowers and freshly baked bread from the market nearby. The village is coming to life, vendors setting up their stalls, and the hum of chatter fills the air. My attention is drawn to a group of children playing near the cobblestone path. One has light red skin that gleams under the sunlight, another's hair is a vibrant blue, bouncing wildly as they laugh, and the smallest among them shifts into a foxe mid-sprint, their copper fur catching the light as they dart between their friends.

I slow my pace, watching the way the children play without a care in the world. It's strange—comforting, even—to see such innocence here, knowing how much unrest and sorrow lies beyond these cabins. Rhadis notices my lingering gaze and follows my line of sight. His lips curve into a small smile, but he doesn't say anything, simply resting a hand on the small of my back to guide me forward.

We reach the diner, a small cabin nestled between two larger shops. It smells of rich coffee and sweet syrup, the kind of place that feels like a warm hug. As we step inside, the waitress looks up from behind the counter and smiles. She's older, her hair streaked with silver, but her movements are quick and efficient as she grabs two menus and leads us to a small wooden table near the window.

"Here you go," she says, placing the menus in front of us. Her gaze flickers to Rhadis, and I can tell she recognizes him for what he is, though she says nothing. Instead, she leans in slightly, lowering her voice. "If you don't mind me saying, you might want to eat with haste. There's word that a God is approaching the market—likely to be here by midday."

I tense, my gaze snapping to hers. "A God?" I ask, my voice steady despite the ripple of unease coursing through me.

She nods, glancing toward the door as if expecting someone to burst in at any moment. "They say he's heading to the neighboring village, looking for a null. Folk are saying he'll pass through here first, though, so best not linger too long."

I glance at Rhadis, whose expression remains calm, though his hand tightens slightly on the edge of the table. "Thank you for the warning," he says, his tone polite but firm, dismissing any further discussion.

The waitress nods and steps away, leaving us alone. I stare at the menu, but my mind is racing. "Still think it's Ymir?" I ask softly, my voice barely above a whisper.

"Likely," Rhadis replies, his gaze fixed on the menu as though we're discussing nothing more pressing than what to order. "But it doesn't change our plans. We'll eat, then see what we can learn from the gossip."

His composure is infuriating, but it also steadies me. If he isn't worried, then I shouldn't be either—or at least that's what I tell myself. I force my attention back to the menu, my eyes scanning the options. Sweetberry cakes catch my eye, and I can't help but smile, the memory of my mother making them for me warming something deep in my chest.

"I'll have the sweetberry cakes," I tell Rhadis as the waitress returns.

He orders Wallrough meat and eggs, his tone as casual as if we were in his castle instead of a village teetering on the edge of danger. As the waitress walks away, I lean forward, lowering my voice. "Do you think the rumor we spread has reached Ymir?"

"I'd bet on it," he says, his expression softening slightly as his gaze meets mine. "It's the kind of story he can't resist—a null, close to giving birth, most likely Emory. He absolutely follows it."

His confidence eases some of my tension, though the thought of Ymir getting closer still sends a chill down my spine. I glance out the window, watching the children still playing in the distance, their laughter a stark contrast to the heaviness settling in my chest.

Rhadis reaches across the table, his fingers brushing mine. "We'll handle it," he says quietly, his voice steady and reassuring. "You're not alone in this."

I nod, squeezing his hand. The food arrives moments later, and I try to focus on the warm, familiar taste of the sweetberry cakes, letting it ground me in the moment. But the waitress's words linger in the back of my mind, a reminder that our peace here is fragile, and Ymir is never far behind.

We finish our meal quickly, though the sweetness of the cakes lingers on my tongue longer than I expect. Rhadis pays, his movements calm and deliberate as always, but I can feel the tension radiating from him, a silent undercurrent beneath his composed exterior. Without a word, he takes my hand, leading me out of the diner and into the bustling market.

The square is alive with activity, vendors calling out their wares and customers bartering loudly. Brightly colored fabrics hang from stalls, their vibrant patterns swaying in the gentle breeze. The scent of roasted nuts and spiced meat fills the air, mixing with the earthy aroma of freshly dug root vegetables. Despite the liveliness, I notice a heaviness in the villagers' eyes, a tension that wasn't as obvious just days before.

Rhadis and I stop at a small apothecary stall first, the shelves lined with tiny glass jars filled with herbs, powders, and tinctures. The woman behind the counter glances up, her expression wary but polite.

"Have you heard the news?" I ask softly, keeping my tone neutral. "About the silver-haired woman?"

She nods, her hands stilling over a jar of dried lavender. "Everyone's talking about it," she whispers, glancing around as if afraid someone might overhear. "He's heading to Ulopia now, isn't he? The God?"

"That's what we've heard," Rhadis says evenly, his voice calm but authoritative. "Do you know if anyone in this village has seen her?"

The woman shakes her head quickly. "No, no one here. But everyone's frightened. His anger... you can feel it, even here. It's like the air's heavier, harder to breathe."

We thank her and move on, stopping at a fabric stall draped with bolts of cloth in every imaginable color. The vendor, a middle-aged man with sharp eyes, repeats the same story—no one's seen the woman, but everyone feels the weight of the god's wrath bearing down on the market.

At the edge of the market, we find a small medical tent. The doctor, a wiry man with sharp cheekbones and a perpetually tired expression, greets us as we step inside. The faint scent of antiseptic mingles with the earthy aroma of herbs hanging from the ceiling.

"I'm looking for the silver-haired woman," I say, keeping my tone light. "We heard she was seen at a medical tent like this one."

The doctor frowns, shaking his head. "I've heard the rumors, but I've never treated anyone like that. I'd remember if I had. A null would be... well, memorable."

Rhadis thanks him, his voice as calm as ever, but I can see the faint tightness in his jaw as we leave. Shop after shop, vendor after vendor, the story is the same. No one here has seen the silver-haired woman, but everyone knows the god is heading to the next village to find her. The fear is palpable, whispered in hurried tones and visible in the wary glances of the villagers.

As we pass a group of children playing near the market's edge, my gaze lingers on them again. Their laughter is soft, tentative now, as if even they can feel the weight pressing down on the village. The smallest, a little girl with curly black hair, tugs at her brother's sleeve, her eyes darting toward us. I feel a pang in my chest, my thoughts immediately flashing to the stolen children I had once nurtured in our cells.

"We can't leave the families in the village to suffer," I say suddenly, my voice firm as I turn to Rhadis. "If Ymir goes there, people are going to get hurt. We need to warn them, get them to leave before it's too late."

Rhadis watches me for a long moment, his expression unreadable. "And where would they go?" he asks quietly. "These people have lived here their entire lives. You can't ask them to abandon everything they've built. This nation is full of creatures and the sand is blistering."

"Lives are more important than homes," I counter, my gaze flicking back to the children. "You can feel it, can't you? His anger —it's getting closer. If he reaches that village and people are still in it, it'll be too late."

His jaw tightens, and for a moment, I think he's going to argue. But then he nods, his shoulders relaxing slightly. "All right," he says. "We'll warn them. But they may not listen."

"They'll listen," I say firmly, though my chest feels tight with doubt. "They have to."

Rhadis's hand brushes against mine, grounding me. "Then let's start."

The sun blazes high in the sky as we move through the closest village from the market, warning every shopkeeper, every family, every soul we can find. Rhadis's voice is steady and authoritative, his words carrying a weight that no one dares to question. I watch as fear flickers in their eyes, followed by determination as they gather their belongings and prepare to leave.

Some families are quick, grabbing only what they can carry and herding their children toward the outskirts of the village. Others hesitate, clutching at keepsakes and memories they can't bear to leave behind. My heart aches as I hear the cries of children who don't understand why they have to go, their small hands tugging at their parents' sleeves, begging to stay.

"Why can't we just hide?" a boy with bright yellow hair asks his mother, his voice trembling as he clutches a stuffed toy.

"Because it's not safe here, love," the mother replies, her voice thick with unshed tears. "We have to keep moving."

I turn away, unable to bear the sight any longer. Rhadis squeezes my hand briefly, his touch grounding me as we move on to the next home. The weight of their fear settles heavily in my chest, but I know we're doing the right thing. They'll be safe, even if it means losing their homes.

By the time the last family has left, the village is eerily silent. The afternoon sun casts long shadows across the empty streets, and the only sounds are the faint rustling of the wind and the distant cries of children as their families disappear into the harsh sands of Ulopia. I stand in the center of the village for a moment, letting the quiet wash over me. It feels... wrong, this emptiness, but it's better than what could have happened.

"We need to hide," Rhadis says softly, his voice pulling me from my thoughts. He nods toward a large tree on the edge of the village, its branches thick enough to conceal us. I follow him, climbing carefully until we're perched high above, the village sprawled out beneath us.

The wait is tense, every moment stretching into eternity. I can feel Rhadis's presence beside me, steady and calm, but my own nerves are fraying. My gaze keeps flicking to the horizon, searching for any sign of him, any movement that might signal his arrival.

And then, he's there.

Ymir strides into the village like a storm, his presence overwhelming even from this distance. His body radiates power, his eyes blazing with anger as he scans the empty streets. For a moment, I think he might leave, that he'll sense the emptiness and move on. But then his rage boils over, suddenly and with seemingly no reason.

With a roar, he lunges at the nearest house, his massive hands tearing through the wooden beams like they're nothing. The walls collapse in on themselves, the sound echoing through the village as splinters and debris scatter. He moves to the next house, and the next, his fury leaving a trail of destruction in its wake.

I press a hand to my mouth, my heart pounding as I watch him rip through homes and livelihoods. The sight is terrifying, but there's also a grim satisfaction in knowing we got the villagers out in time. No one is here to face his wrath, to be caught in the storm of his anger.

Rhadis remains silent beside me, his gaze locked on Ymir, his expression unreadable. I glance at him, searching for some sign of what he's thinking, but he gives nothing away. His hand brushes against mine briefly, a silent reassurance, though I can see the tension in his shoulders.

When Ymir finally leaves, the village is unrecognizable. Homes have been reduced to rubble, the once merchant stalls lie in splinters, and the streets are littered with debris. He stalks off into the distance, his anger still palpable even as his figure disappears into the horizon.

I let out a shaky breath, my hands trembling as I cling to the branch beneath me. "We did the right thing," I whisper, more to myself than to Rhadis. "They're safe."

"They are," Rhadis agrees, his voice low and steady. "For now."

We climb down from the tree carefully, the silence of the village pressing down on us like a heavy weight. I take one last look at the ruins, my chest tight with a mix of relief and sadness.

We saved them, but at what cost? This village will never be the same.

"Come on," Rhadis says gently, his hand resting lightly on my back. "We need to keep moving."

I nod, swallowing the lump in my throat as we turn away from the destruction and start toward the horizon.

The air is heavy as Rhadis sets the tent back up on a patch of soft, dry ground just beyond the ruined village. His movements are efficient, methodical, though I can see the tension lingering in his shoulders. The shadows from his skin seep into the fabric as he works, and within moments, the structure changes.

What was once a simple tent becomes another small cabin, even smaller than the last. This one is compact, just a cot pushed against one wall and a tiny adjoining room that I assume is the outhouse. There's no hearth this time, no counter or chairs, just enough space for us to rest.

He steps back, surveying his work before turning to me. "It's not much," he says, his voice low. "But it'll do for tonight."

I nod, my fingers brushing over the edge of the doorframe. "It's perfect," I murmur, though my attention lingers on him. The way he carries himself, the tension in his jaw—it's clear his mind is elsewhere.

As if sensing my thoughts, Rhadis glances at me, his dark eyes sharp yet distant. "I felt something," he says suddenly, his voice quieter now. "A ripple, just before Ymir destroyed the village."

I blink, stepping closer to him. "A ripple? What do you mean?"

His gaze softens slightly, though the weight of his words remains heavy. "It was brief, but unmistakable. The curse Emory carried—it's broken. I'm certain of it."

The words hit me like a wave, and my breath catches. "Then that means…"

He nods. "Her child has been born. The fates have shifted."

A warmth blooms in my chest at the thought of Emory holding her baby, of the curse that has haunted her for the last seven months finally being lifted. But the weight of what we've just witnessed pulls me back.

"Do you think Ymir is far enough away now?" I ask cautiously. "That we could return to the underworld?"

Rhadis considers this, his gaze distant as if he's searching for something just beyond our reach. Finally, he nods. "Yes. He's far enough. We'll return in a week, after ensuring he does not hurt any villagers as he searches."

Relief floods through me, and I reach out to touch his arm. "Good," I say softly. "I want to see her. To see them."

He nods again, his expression softening for a moment as he places his hand over mine. "We will. But tonight, we rest and tomorrow we work."

I glance at the cot, my lips twitching into a small smile. "That doesn't look big enough for both of us."

His smirk returns, faint but familiar. "We'll manage," he says, his voice carrying a hint of teasing. "Unless you'd prefer to sleep outside."

I roll my eyes, but the tension in my chest eases slightly as I follow him into the cabin. The space is tight, the cot barely large enough for one person, let alone two, but it feels safe. Cozy, even.

Rhadis sets his sword within reach, his movements deliberate as he prepares for the night. I watch him for a moment, the steady rhythm of his actions grounding me. Despite everything —Ymir's destruction, the uncertainty that lies ahead—there's a quiet strength in him that makes me feel like we can face anything.

As I settle onto the cot, Rhadis sits beside me, his hand brushing against mine. "In one week," he murmurs, his voice low and certain, "we'll go home."

Home. The word carries a weight I hadn't realized I was holding, and for the first time in days, I feel a sense of peace. I nod, leaning into him as his arm wraps around my shoulders. Whatever comes next, we'll face it together.

CHAPTER FOURTEEN

The first soft rays of dawn filter into our newest cabin, casting faint shadows on the walls. I stir, my head still resting against Rhadis's bare chest. The steady rhythm of his breathing tells me he's still asleep, his arm draped protectively around my waist. For a moment, I just watch him, the peaceful expression on his face a stark contrast to the intensity he carries when awake.

I can't resist leaning forward, pressing a gentle kiss to his jawline. His skin is warm, and the faint stubble tickles my lips. He stirs, a low groan rumbling in his chest as his arm tightens around me, pulling me closer. His eyes flutter open, the glowing red ring in his pupils faint but present as he focuses on me.

"Morning," he murmurs, his voice rough with sleep.

"Morning," I whisper back, smiling as I press another kiss to his jaw.

He grumbles softly, his arm shifting to cradle the back of my head as he holds me against him. I can feel the hardness of him pressing against my thigh, but he doesn't move to do anything more. Instead, he just holds me, his hand sliding gently up and down my back in a way that feels both protective and tender.

I bury my face in the crook of his neck, savoring the warmth of him. Eventually, though, he shifts, his muscles flexing as he stretches. "Time to get up," he says, his voice steadier now. "We've got to pack and head back."

I groan softly, reluctant to move, but I nod. Sliding out of the cot, I begin gathering our things, folding the furs and packing the few items we've used during our stay at this cabin. Rhadis stands, stretching again before stepping outside to dismantle the cabin. I watch as the shadows seep from his hands, the structure shrinking back into the original tent. He folds it with practiced ease, slipping it into one of the bags before turning to me.

"Ready?" he asks, his dark eyes meeting mine.

I nod, slinging one of the smaller bags over my shoulder. He smirks, reaching out to take it from me and add it to his own load. "Close your eyes," he says.

I do as he asks, the familiar tingling of his magic brushing against my skin. When I open my eyes, the castle looms before us, it's dark stone walls standing tall and imposing against the morning sky. The sight of it fills me with a sense of relief, the weight of the past few days lifting slightly as I step toward home.

Rhadis leads the way inside, his stride confident and purposeful. As we enter the main hall, Helic is waiting for us, his expression calm but his eyes alight with news.

“My lord, my lady,” Helic says with a bow, “the child has been born. The fates have shifted. They have named the boy Atlas.”

Rhadis nods, his hand brushing against the small of my back as he guides me toward the dining hall. My heart swells at the thought of Emory and her new child, now only a week old, though I push aside the urge to run straight to her room. Breakfast first, I remind myself. Then we’ll see them.

Rhadis pulls out my chair at the dining table, pushing it in gently after I sit. As usual, he takes the seat at the head of the table, his presence commanding even in this quiet moment. The room is empty for now, the rest of the castle still waking, but I know it won’t be long before everyone joins us.

I glance at Rhadis, who sits with his usual composed demeanor, his fingers steepled as he waits. His gaze meets mine, and for a moment, his expression softens, a quiet warmth passing between us. Whatever happens next, we’re home, and we’re together. That’s all that matters.

The warmth of his touch doesn’t alleviate the unease curling in my stomach, but it steadies me enough to focus on the conversation. Around the table, the chatter fades as people settle into their seats, the weight of what we all know is coming hanging heavily in the air.

“Look who finally decided to join us,” Rhadis drawls, his deep voice cutting through the quiet. His dark eyes land on Atlas, bundled in Emory’s arms, and for a fleeting moment, his sharp features soften. “And look at the little heir. Already growing fast at only a week old.”

Emory smiles as she takes her seat, her movements careful, almost protective. There's exhaustion in her expression, but her eyes are warm as she glances down at her son. I watch the way Ryat pulls out a chair for her, his hand brushing hers before he sits beside her, his dark gaze scanning the room.

"How was the journey?" Emory asks, her voice tinged with curiosity and concern. "What did you find?"

I glance at Rhadis before answering, choosing my words carefully. "It went as well as it could," I say, my tone even. "We kept him away—for now."

Ryat leans forward slightly, his elbows resting on the table as he focuses on me. "How did you manage it?" he asks, his voice laced with tension. "How did you keep him off your trail?"

"Rumors," I reply simply, meeting his gaze. "We spread them in every village we could reach, making sure that every lead he found pointed him in the wrong direction."

Emory's brow furrows as she looks between me and Rhadis. "And it worked?" she asks, a note of uncertainty in her voice.

Rhadis leans back in his chair, his fingers tapping idly against the armrest. "For now," he says, his tone edged with caution. "But it won't last. Ymir isn't a fool. Eventually, he'll realize what's happening."

The room falls silent, the weight of his words sinking in. My gaze shifts to Atlas, his tiny form a stark reminder of why we're all here, why we can't afford to fail. Emory cradles him closer, her lips pressing into a thin line.

"And when he does?" Ryat asks, his voice low but steady.

Rhadis straightens in his seat, his expression darkening. "Then he'll come for us. With everything he has."

A shiver runs down my spine, and I can't stop myself from reaching for Rhadis's hand, my fingers curling around his. He glances at me, his gaze softening for a brief moment before he continues. "The curse breaking has only made him more dangerous. He feels the prophecy unraveling, and it's pushing him further into rage."

Emory's voice breaks through the silence, quiet but firm. "What happened when the curse broke? What did he do?"

I hesitate, the memory of that destroyed village flashing in my mind. Rhadis is the one who answers. "He trashed an entire village," he says bluntly. "Homes, businesses… he tore it all apart with his bare hands. Luckily, the villagers were evacuated in time, but the damage…" He trails off, shaking his head.

Emory's eyes widen, her face pale as she looks at Atlas, then back at Rhadis. "Because of me?" she whispers, her voice trembling.

"No," I say firmly, leaning forward. "It's because of him. His choices, his anger. None of this is your fault."

Ryat's hand covers hers, his grip steady. "Raya's right," he says softly. "Ymir's actions are his own. You're not responsible for the destruction he caused."

Emory nods slowly, but the guilt doesn't leave her eyes. "What do we do now?" she asks, her voice barely above a whisper.

Rhadis's gaze hardens, his tone sharp with determination. "We prepare. If we wait for him to come to us, we'll lose the advantage. We need to act first."

The room grows quieter still as everyone processes his words. Eira is the first to speak, her voice steady despite the uncertainty in her expression. "What happens if we succeed? If Ymir is defeated?"

Rhadis's tone softens slightly, though it remains firm. "The curse will break completely. The lands he's held under his control, the prophecy—everything will be undone."

Emory's grip on Atlas tightens, her gaze dropping to her son. "And if we don't succeed?" she whispers, her voice barely audible.

"We will," Ryat says firmly, his voice filled with quiet conviction. "We have to."

I glance at Rhadis, his dark eyes meeting mine. His resolve is unshakable, but I can see the weight he carries, the responsibility pressing down on him like a physical force. Without thinking, I squeeze his hand, offering the only reassurance I can.

"We'll do whatever it takes," I say softly, my voice steady. "For all of us."

Rhadis nods, his expression grim but resolute. "Then we start planning."

As the conversation shifts to strategy, I can't help but glance around the room, at the faces of the people I've come to call family. There's fear in their eyes, but also hope. And for the first time in a long while, I feel like we might actually have a chance.

CHAPTER FIFTEEN

The sun is high in the sky, casting warm light over the training grounds. The air smells of earth and sweat, a reminder of the long hours we've spent preparing for the final battle. Teirney stands across from me, her stance confident, her twin blades glinting in the light. I grip my sword tightly, adjusting my footing as we circle each other, neither willing to make the first move.

"You're not going to go easy on me, are you?" I ask, a small smirk tugging at my lips.

Teirney grins, her long black hair catching the sunlight. "Not a chance."

She moves first, darting forward with a quick slash aimed at my side. I parry it, the clash of our blades ringing out across the grounds. Her speed is impressive, but I've sparred with her enough to anticipate her moves. She pivots, bringing her second blade around in a sweeping arc, but I step back just in time, the blade slicing through the air where I stood moments ago.

"Too slow," I taunt, though my heart is pounding in my chest.

Teirney narrows her eyes, her grin sharpening. She lunges again, her strikes faster this time, more calculated. I meet her blade for blade, the clash of steel reverberating through my arms. Sweat beads on my brow as we move, our dance one of precision and instinct. She's relentless, and I have to admit, she's keeping me on my toes.

I feint to the left, then bring my blade around to her right, aiming for her unprotected side. She blocks it with a quick twist of her wrist, her other blade coming dangerously close to my shoulder. I duck, rolling to the side and coming up with my sword ready. Teirney is on me again in an instant, her strikes aggressive but controlled.

The fight continues, neither of us gaining the upper hand. My muscles burn with exertion, but I don't let up. Teirney is a skilled opponent, and I respect her too much to hold back. Finally, she steps back, lowering her blades with a breathless laugh.

"Good," she says, wiping sweat from her brow. "You're faster than the last time we spared."

I lower my sword, my chest heaving as I catch my breath. "And you're stronger," I reply, a genuine smile breaking across my face. "Your counters are better too. I need to work on anticipating them."

Teirney nods, handing me a waterskin. "And I need to stop favoring my right side so much. You almost had me there."

We sit for a moment, sharing the water and discussing our

techniques, pointing out each other's strengths and weaknesses. It's a calm, thoughtful exchange, one that reminds me how much I've come to appreciate her sharp mind and even sharper skills.

After a while, I stand, my muscles aching but my spirits high. "I'm going to check on Atlas," I say, glancing toward the other end of the training grounds.

Teirney waves me off with a grin. "Don't let him charm you too much, you spoil him."

I laugh, already walking toward Arden, who is standing under a shaded tree with Atlas cradled in his arms. The baby boy is babbling happily, one chubby hand tugging at Arden's shirt while the other waves in the air.

"There's my favorite little troublemaker," I coo as I reach them, holding my arms out.

Arden chuckles, carefully transferring Atlas into my arms. "He's been blabbering up a storm," he says. "Not that I understand a lick of it."

I cuddle Atlas close, pressing a kiss to his soft silver hair. "That's because he's a genius, and we mere mortals can't comprehend his wisdom."

Atlas babbles again, his bright eyes crinkling with laughter as I nuzzle his cheek. I settle onto the grass, leaning back against the tree as I hold him. He tugs at my braid, his tiny fingers surprisingly strong, and I can't help but smile.

"Your mama is amazing, you know that?" I murmur, watching

as Emory spars with Rhadis across the training grounds. Her movements are fluid, her sword flashing in the light as she matches Rhadis strike for strike. "She's so strong, so brave. She's almost ready, little one. Almost there."

Atlas giggles, his laughter like a balm to my weary heart. I bounce him gently in my arms, his joy infectious as I watch his mom and my mate. Emory's determination is evident in every swing of her blade, and Rhadis's focus is unwavering as he pushes her to improve. It's a sight that fills me with pride—and a fierce hope for what's to come.

"You're going to grow up in a safer world," I whisper to Atlas, my voice soft but firm. "Because your mama, papa and all of your family are going to make sure of it."

He coos in response, his tiny hands reaching for my face, and I laugh, holding him close as I let the moment wash over me.

Once the day turns chilly, a bit of winter still hanging in the air, we head inside to continue. The indoor training room buzzes with activity, the energy in the air charged with purpose. The sounds of weapons clashing, arrows thudding into targets, and bursts of elemental power create a symphony of preparation.

I stand beside Nox, the weight of my bow in my hands familiar and grounding. His dark eyes flick to me as he adjusts the tension on his own bowstring, a faint smile tugging at his lips. "You ready?" he asks, his voice steady.

"Always," I reply, lifting my bow and nocking an arrow. My gaze locks onto the target across the room, the red circle painted boldly against the pale wood. I draw back the string, feeling the tension hum through my fingers, and release. The arrow sails through the air, embedding itself just shy of the center.

"Close," Nox remarks, letting his own arrow fly and hitting dead center with ease. "But you're hesitating. Focus on the release."

I huff, narrowing my eyes at the target as I reach for another arrow. "Maybe I'm just trying to make you feel better about your aim."

He chuckles, his smirk widening. "Sure, let's go with that."

Beside us, Hellion and Eira are practicing their gifts, their movements fluid and precise. Hellion's fire gift is intense, flames dancing along his fingers as he controls them with practiced ease. He shapes a roaring flame into a tight spiral, sending it shooting across the room where it dissipates harmlessly against a stone barrier.

Eira's water gift is just as impressive, if not more so. She holds her hands out, and water flows effortlessly from her palms, forming into intricate shapes. She pulls the water into a sphere, compressing it until it's no bigger than her fist, then sends it shooting toward the same barrier. The force of the water sends droplets scattering, glinting like diamonds in the air.

I can't help but watch, mesmerized by the sheer power and control she displays. The way she commands the water is almost hypnotic, the fluidity and precision of her movements leaving me in awe.

"Raya," Nox says sharply, his voice breaking through my thoughts. "Focus."

I blink, realizing I've lowered my bow. "Sorry," I mutter, feeling my cheeks heat as I lift it again.

Nox smirks, but his tone remains encouraging. "She's impressive, sure, but distractions won't help you hit your mark."

I nod, drawing back the string once more. This time, I take a deep breath, centering myself as I line up the shot. The arrow flies true, striking the target just to the right of the bullseye. It's not perfect, but it's better.

"Better," Nox says, his voice carrying a note of approval. "Now keep it up."

As we continue practicing, the room hums with focused determination. Hellion and Eira push each other, their gifts clashing in bursts of steam as fire meets water. Rhadis and Emory spar in the corner, their movements sharp and deliberate, the clang of their swords echoing in the space.

Despite the intensity of the training, there's a sense of camaraderie in the room, an unspoken understanding that we're all working toward the same goal. It's a reminder of what we're fighting for, of the lives we're trying to protect.

I glance at Atlas, who is sitting in a makeshift playpen near the edge of the room, babbling happily as Fenor keeps a watchful eye on him. The sight of his bright silver hair and wide, curious eyes fills me with a renewed sense of purpose.

This battle will be the hardest we've ever faced, but we're ready. We have to be.

CHAPTER SIXTEEN

The dining hall is quieter than usual, the weight of the approaching battle pressing down on all of us. The long table is lined with familiar faces, their expressions tense as the air crackles with unspoken questions. Even the pups, Layken and Kalleli, seem subdued, curled up at Emory's feet as if sensing the gravity of the moment.

Rhadis sits at the head of the table, his dark eyes sweeping over us as we eat in near silence. I feel the tension radiating from him and place a steadying hand on his arm. He gives me a brief nod before clearing his throat, breaking the silence.

"I need to address something before the battle," he begins, his deep voice carrying through the room with ease. All eyes turn to him, the clinking of silverware falling silent. "The fates have made it clear to me that I cannot participate in the destruction of Ymir."

There's a collective pause, followed by murmurs of confusion and disbelief. My heart skips at his words, my grip on his arm tightening slightly.

"What do you mean?" Ryat asks, his tone sharp but measured. "You're the God of the Underworld. Surely you—"

Rhadis raises a hand to stop him, his expression unreadable. "It's not a matter of power, Ryat. It's the fates' will. I've been told I cannot involve myself directly in this battle against another God."

Emory shifts uneasily in her seat, her hand resting protectively on her son, Atlas, who's seated on her lap. "So what does this mean for us?" she asks, her voice steady but laced with concern.

Rhadis leans forward, his fingers steepled as he looks around the table. "It means that while I cannot fight, I will do everything in my power to ensure you have the best chance of success. However, there are decisions that must be made regarding who will go and who will stay behind."

His gaze flicks around the table, landing on me before moving to Eira. I feel the shift before he even says the words, the pit in my stomach growing heavier.

"I've decided that Eira and Raya will stay behind to care for Atlas."

"What?" The word escapes me before I can stop it, sharp and incredulous. I straighten in my chair, my heart pounding. "You're not serious."

Rhadis looks at me, his expression calm but firm. "I am. The child needs protection. If we fail, someone must be here to ensure his safety."

I clench my fists, the frustration rising in my chest like a tide. "You can't ask me to stay behind, Rhadis. You can't ask me to sit here and do nothing while everyone else—"

"It's not nothing," he interrupts, his voice steady but unyielding. "Protecting Atlas is just as important as the battle itself. You are his shield, Raya. Just as Eira is."

The room feels like it's spinning, the weight of his words pressing down on me. I glance at Eira, who looks conflicted but nods, her dark eyes filled with quiet determination. "I'll do it," she says softly. "I'll stay and care for him."

My gaze shifts to Emory, desperate for her support. But she's holding Atlas close, her expression torn. When her eyes meet mine, there's something in them that breaks me—a silent understanding, a plea. She's counting on me.

I swallow hard, turning back to Rhadis. "I don't want to lose you," I say quietly, my voice trembling with frustration and something I can't name. "I don't want to stand by and let you—"

"You're not going to lose me," he says, his tone softening as his hand covers mine. "You're protecting what we've built. What Emory and Ryat have built. That's just as important as wielding a blade."

His words settle over me, heavy and suffocating. I hate it. I hate the logic in his voice, the way he's right, the way I can't argue. I look down at my hands, my chest tight with frustration and fear.

"I'll stay," I say finally, the words bitter on my tongue. "But only because I trust you and love my nephew."

His hand tightens over mine, a quiet reassurance. "That's all I ask."

The conversation shifts, the others discussing their roles and strategies. But I stay quiet, my mind spinning, my chest aching. I glance at Atlas, now reaching for a piece of bread on the table, and my resolve strengthens. For him, for Emory, I'll stay. But I can't shake the fear twisting in my gut—that I'll lose Rhadis, and I won't be there to stop it.

Rhadis leans back in his chair, his hand resting on the table as his sharp gaze sweeps across the room. The atmosphere is thick with tension, every word he speaks weighing heavier than the last. I sit silently beside him, my heart twisting as he continues to lay out the plan, his voice steady and commanding.

"There's one more thing," he says, his tone quieting the murmurs that had started around the table. "Hellion and Azrael will not join the main fight."

Both men immediately stiffen. Hellion, with his fiery presence that always seems just barely contained, narrows his eyes, leaning forward. "What are you talking about?" His voice is low, his frustration obvious. "You need us in that battle."

Rhadis shakes his head, his expression unyielding. "No. Your powers are too dangerous in a confrontation like this. Ymir cannot know you are there. If he senses either of you, he will turn his focus on you, and the risk is too high."

Azrael crosses his arms, his jaw tight. "So what are we supposed to do? Sit around and wait for everyone else to fall?"

Rhadis's gaze sharpens, a flicker of his shadows curling along the edges of his chair. "You are the fallback. If things go wrong —if the rest of the group falls—you two will step in and ensure Ymir's defeat. But until that moment, you remain hidden. The realm, the child, everyone will need you at full strength if the rest of the group cannot beat him."

Hellion exhales sharply, running a hand through his dark hair, clearly frustrated. "I don't like it. We could end this faster if we were in the fight from the start."

"You could also endanger everything we've planned," Rhadis counters, his voice calm but firm. "Ymir doesn't know you're here, and that's our greatest advantage. If the rest of the group can weaken him without revealing your presence, the final blow will be all the more effective."

Azrael shifts uncomfortably, his expression still tense. "And if the group doesn't weaken him?"

"Then you adapt," Rhadis says simply. "But you'll have the element of surprise, and that will be critical."

I glance at Hellion and Azrael, their frustration palpable, but they don't argue further. I can see the struggle in their eyes, the desire to protect their friends clashing with the reality of the plan. It's not an easy decision for any of them.

Rhadis reaches for my hand under the table, his grip firm but comforting. I glance at him, his red-ringed eyes meeting mine briefly before he turns back to the group. "This isn't an easy decision, but it's the right one. We need to trust the fates, trust the plan."

The room falls into a heavy silence, the weight of his words settling over everyone. Emory glances at Ryat, her silver hair catching the light, her expression pensive. Vor looks as though he's already strategizing, his sharp mind working through the details.

Finally, Hellion nods, though his frustration is still evident. "Fine. We'll stay hidden. But if things start to fall apart, we're stepping in."

"That's all I ask," Rhadis replies, his voice steady.

The tension eases slightly, though it doesn't disappear entirely. I feel Rhadis's grip on my hand tighten briefly, a quiet reassurance that steadies me even as the fear of what's to come lingers in my chest. I know the stakes are high, and every decision made tonight could mean the difference between victory and devastation.

CHAPTER SEVENTEEN

I sit on the edge of the training room, sharpening yet another blade, the rhythmic scrape of the whetstone grounding me. Across the room, Emory and Rhadis spar, their movements a dance of steel and precision. Emory's silver hair is damp, strands sticking to her face as she counters each of Rhadis's strikes with growing confidence. His dark presence looms over her, his movements deliberate, commanding, yet he's holding back just enough to test her without overwhelming her.

She meets him strike for strike, her blade flashing as she pushes herself harder, faster. I can't help but feel pride watching her. She's come so far from the woman I first met—stronger, fiercer, ready for what's to come. But the sight of Rhadis across from her, the way he moves with an almost predatory grace, sends a shiver through me. He's a god, after all, and his power seeps into the air like a shadow.

Their sparring match ends abruptly. Rhadis steps back, lowering his blade, and studies her for a long moment. His sharp gaze takes her in, every breath she draws, every bead of sweat trailing down her skin.

"You're ready," he says finally, his voice low and steady, carrying a weight that seems to settle over the room.

Emory blinks, her chest heaving as she catches her breath. For a moment, she doesn't respond, and then she nods, a flicker of determination lighting her eyes. I try to focus on my blade as he tells her to prepare her things and that he will keep an eye on Atlas as she does so.

Rhadis's gaze follows her for a moment before he turns, his attention landing on me. I focus back on the blade in my hands, pretending I wasn't just watching them. But I can feel him moving toward me, his presence as tangible as the shadows he commands.

He sets his sword down on the table beside me and takes the blade from my hands, inspecting it briefly before placing it aside as well. Then, without warning, he pulls me to my feet, his hands firm but gentle as they settle on my waist.

"You've been quiet," he says, his voice soft, almost teasing.

I glance up at him, my heart fluttering at the intensity in his gaze. "Just thinking," I say quietly, my hands resting lightly on his chest.

He tilts his head, studying me. "About?"

"About how soon you'll all be leaving," I admit, my voice barely above a whisper. "And how I'll have to stay behind, waiting."

His expression softens, the sharpness in his eyes giving way to something warmer, something deeper. He pulls me closer, resting his chin on top of my head. "I'll be waiting too," he murmurs. "And I'll be counting every second until we're back together."

I close my eyes, letting myself sink into the warmth of him, the safety he provides. "I'll miss you," I whisper.

He pulls back just enough to look at me, his lips quirking into a smirk that I know all too well. "You'll miss me, huh?" he teases, his voice lighter now. "Or are you going to miss my tongue and cock?"

The heat rushes to my face so fast I feel like I might combust. "Rhadis," I hiss, swatting at his chest, though the laughter bubbling up betrays me.

He grins, unrepentant, and pulls me even closer. "I'm serious," he says, his voice dropping to a softer, more intimate tone. "I'm going to miss you too. Every second I'm out there."

My heart clenches at his words, and I swallow hard, my fingers curling against his chest. "I know," I say softly, my voice steady despite the emotions threatening to overwhelm me.

For a moment, we just stand there, wrapped in each other. The weight of what's coming presses against us, unspoken but understood. And in this quiet moment, I let myself believe that we'll both make it through. Together.

I stay in the smaller training room, the faint hum of voices from the main hall filtering through the stone walls. I can't bring myself to join them just yet. Knowing that this is the last time I'll see Rhadis for what feels like an eternity—it's too much. I need this moment, this quiet space where it's just us.

Rhadis stands in front of me, his dark eyes studying my face as if committing every detail to memory. I grip his hands tightly, my thumbs tracing the lines of his knuckles. He doesn't speak, and neither do I. The weight of everything we haven't said hangs between us, but words don't feel necessary.

He lifts one of my hands to his lips, pressing a kiss to my fingers before pulling me into his arms. His embrace is warm, solid, and I let myself melt into him, resting my cheek against his chest. The steady rhythm of his heartbeat grounds me, but it doesn't ease the ache in my chest.

"You're quiet," he murmurs, his voice low and soothing.

I close my eyes, tightening my arms around him. "I'm just... trying to make this moment last."

His hand strokes my back, his touch light but deliberate. "I'm not going anywhere unsafe," he says softly. "Not really. I'll be here soon."

I tilt my head up to look at him, my throat tightening at the sincerity in his gaze. "You can't promise that," I whisper. "Not with what's coming. You may not be able to hurt him, but we do not know if the fates have told him the same of you."

His expression hardens slightly, his jaw clenching. "Yes, I can," he says firmly. "Because I refuse to let this end any other way."

I want to believe him, but the fear gnawing at me won't let

go. "Rhadis, you can't control everything. And if something happens—"

He silences me with a kiss, his lips capturing mine in a way that leaves no room for argument. It's not a kiss of passion but of reassurance, a vow wrapped in the quiet strength that only he possesses. When he pulls back, his forehead rests against mine, his hands cradling my face.

"You are my mate, my heart, my everything," he says quietly, his voice steady and unshakable. "I will protect this realm, but I will not leave it without you."

The tears I've been holding back finally spill over, and I bury my face in his chest, my fingers clutching his shirt. He doesn't try to stop them, doesn't tell me it's going to be okay again—he just holds me, letting me feel everything without judgment.

Minutes pass, or maybe hours—I don't know. Time feels irrelevant when I'm wrapped in him, in this moment. But eventually, the sound of voices growing louder in the main hall reminds me that the others are waiting, that time is slipping away.

I pull back slightly, wiping at my cheeks. "I just... I hate that I can't go with you. That I can't fight beside everyone."

Rhadis cups my chin, tilting my face up so I'm forced to meet his gaze. "You are fighting, Raya," he says softly. "By staying here and protecting Atlas, you're fighting. You're ensuring there's something to come back to."

I nod, even though the words don't ease the ache in my chest.

"Just come back to me," I whisper.

"I will," he says simply, as if there's no other option.

He kisses me one last time, and then the door creaks open, and Fenors voice cuts through the air.

"Raya? We're almost ready to leave."

I glance over my shoulder, nodding at him before turning back to Rhadis. I take a shaky breath, letting myself look at him one last time before stepping back. He doesn't let go of my hand until I'm too far for him to hold on.

And then, with a heavy heart, I follow Fenor into the main hall, leaving a piece of myself behind.

CHAPTER SEVENTEEN

I'm lying on the floor, propped up on my elbows as I dangle a wooden foxe in front of Atlas. His tiny hands reach for it, his giggles bright and infectious as he tries to grab it. Eira sits nearby, twirling a small water orb between her fingers, her attention half on Atlas and half on the game she's playing with her power.

Atlas squeals as his chubby fingers finally latch onto the toy, pulling it close to his chest like it's his greatest treasure. His silver hair glints in the soft sunlight streaming through the windows, and I can't help but smile at him, at how pure and untouched by all of this he is.

"You're going to spoil him with all this attention," Eira teases, her voice light.

I chuckle, scooping Atlas into my lap and kissing the top of his head. "He deserves it. It's a rough world out there—he should have all the love we can give him."

Eira nods, her smile softening. "You're right about that."

The moment feels peaceful, almost normal—until it happens.

A ripple cuts through the air, sharp and cold, like the aftershock of something immense and dark. The room seems to shudder with it, a faint tremor that's not physical but deeply felt, as if the very fabric of the world is reacting to whatever just happened.

Atlas's giggles turn into wails, his small body trembling against me. My heart clenches as I hold him closer, rocking him gently and whispering soothing words into his hair. "Shh, baby," I murmur, rocking him gently as I press kisses to his soft silver hair. "It's okay. You're safe. I've got you."

Eira is on her feet instantly, her water orb dissipating as her attention snaps to the window. She doesn't speak at first, her brows furrowing as she looks out at the horizon, her posture tense.

Her usual calm demeanor is gone, replaced by a growing unease that mirrors my own. The ripple is gone, but its presence lingers like a shadow, a faint hum in the air that refuses to settle.

"What was that?" she asks, her voice tight and urgent.

I bounce Atlas slightly, my hands rubbing small circles on his back as I try to calm him. His wails soften into broken cries, his tiny body still shaking. "I don't know," I say quietly, my voice trembling. "It felt... wrong. Like something powerful just happened."

Eira turns to me, her dark eyes filled with questions she doesn't want to voice. "Do you think... Do you think they won?"

I hesitate, my gaze falling to Atlas's face. His cheeks are red from crying, his little lips quivering as he hiccups against me. I press my cheek to his, closing my eyes as I try to push back the fear clawing at my chest. "I don't know," I whisper. "It could mean anything."

Eira crosses the room, her steps quick but silent, and places a hand on my shoulder. Her grip is firm, grounding, but I can see the worry etched into her face. "Raya," she says softly, her tone laced with concern. "What do you feel?"

I glance at her, swallowing hard. "I feel..." My voice falters, and I shake my head. "I don't know. It's like the air shifted. Darker, heavier. But... I can't tell if it's good or bad."

Atlas stirs against me, his tiny fingers clutching at my shirt, and I look down at him, my heart aching at how fragile he feels in my arms. His cries have quieted, but his breathing is uneven, his body still tense. "It's okay, little one," I murmur, kissing his temple. "We won't let anything hurt you."

Eira kneels beside me, her hand brushing lightly against Atlas's back. "He felt it too," she says softly. "Whatever that was... it was big."

I nod, my throat tight. "I just hope... I hope it means they're coming back. All of them."

Eira doesn't say anything, but the look in her eyes tells me she's hoping for the same. The silence stretches between us, heavy and unyielding, as we wait for answers that may never come.

CHAPTER EIGHTEEN

I cradle Atlas in my arms, nuzzling his soft silver hair as I joke softly, "You've got the stinkiest diapers in the realm, you know that? No wonder your auntie keeps saying I spoil you—I just want to get you fresh and clean." He gurgles up at me, his tiny fingers grabbing at my braid as I laugh and finish changing him.

"There, now you smell like the sweet little prince you are," I say, kissing his tiny forehead. I wrap him snugly in a fur, preparing to settle him into his crib when I hear the commotion. It's faint at first, muffled voices and hurried footsteps from downstairs, but it's enough to send a ripple of worry through me.

My heart stutters. Something is wrong.

"Come on, sweet boy," I whisper, pressing Atlas closer to me as I hurry out of the room and down the stairs. The noise grows louder with every step, the clatter of boots, frantic voices overlapping. When I reach the entryway, the sight before me makes my blood run cold.

They're back—but they look destroyed.

Ryat is at the center of the group, cradling Emory's unconscious form in his arms. Her face is pale, her silver hair matted with blood, and she looks so still it makes my chest ache. His jaw is tight, his eyes blazing with barely-contained fear as he carries her toward the stairs.

Nearby, Haven is slumped against the wall, her face and arms covered in bruises, her once-pristine armor dented and smeared with dirt. Vor leans heavily against her, his clothing torn and blood-soaked, deep gashes visible along his arms and torso.

Fenris is on a makeshift stretcher, his chest rising and falling faintly as if each breath takes monumental effort. His face is ghostly pale, his usually vibrant energy nowhere to be found. And then I see him—Fenor.

Rhadis is carrying him, my brother's limp body cradled against his chest like he weighs nothing. Fenor's face is bloodied, his skin deathly pale, and his breaths are so shallow I can barely see his chest move. My heart lurches, and without thinking, I rush forward.

"Fenor!" My voice cracks as I reach Rhadis, my free hand flying to my brother's face. His skin is icy, his usual warmth gone, and I feel my stomach twist painfully. "Is he okay? Rhadis, tell me he's okay."

Rhadis's eyes meet mine, his gaze shadowed and intense. "He's alive, but barely," he says, his voice low and steady. "We need to get him treated—now."

Holic is already rushing toward us with a medical kit, his face grim as he begins barking orders. "Lay them out in the sitting room! I need space to work!" He gestures to the side, directing Rhadis, Ryat, and the others to place their injured down.

I follow as Rhadis moves, every step feeling like a battle against the panic clawing at my throat. "Fenor, you have to stay with me," I whisper, my hand still on his face, my voice trembling. "You hear me? You can't leave me when I just got you back."

Rhadis gently lays Fenor on a chaise, his movements careful despite the urgency in his expression. "Raya," he says softly, pulling me back slightly, "he's strong. He'll fight."

I nod, though tears blur my vision as I step back, still clutching Atlas tightly to my chest. "He has to."

Holic is already assessing injuries, his hands swift and efficient as he moves from Fenor to Fenris, then to Vor and Haven. He pauses briefly at Emory, his brow furrowing as he checks her pulse. "She's alive," he says, glancing at Ryat, whose expression doesn't change as he lowers her onto a couch.

"What happened?" I manage to ask, my voice barely above a whisper. My gaze flicks to Ryat, who looks as battered as the rest of them but stands firm, his focus entirely on Emory.

Ryat finally speaks, his voice hoarse and heavy with exhaustion. "We fought Ymir," he says simply, his tone clipped. "It was... chaos."

"And Ymir?" I ask, my stomach twisting.

"He's dead," Rhadis answers, his voice steady and certain. "Emory unraveled him."

My gaze snaps to him. "She did it?"

Rhadis nods. "She gave everything she had. That ripple we felt earlier—that was the moment she broke him." His eyes darken, glancing toward Emory's unconscious form. "But it took everything out of her."

Tears prick my eyes as I look back at Fenor. "And Fenor? Fenris? Everyone else?"

"We all fought," Haven interjects weakly, her voice raspy as she leans against Vor. "But Ymir's powers weren't just strong—they were ever growing. Fenor took the brunt of an attack protecting Fenris. Fenris burned through his life force healing everyone else."

"And Vor?" I whisper, glancing at him.

Vor shrugs, wincing as the movement pulls at his injuries. "Too slow with my sword," he mutters. "Got slashed a few times. I'll live."

I exhale shakily, rocking Atlas as he stirs against me, his small whimpers pulling me back to the present. Rhadis's hand brushes my arm, grounding me, and I glance up at him, finding comfort in his steady presence.

"We'll take care of them," Rhadis says quietly, his voice low but firm. "All of them."

I nod, clinging to his words as Holic moves among the injured, barking more orders. There's so much blood, so much pain, but they're here. They're alive. For now, I think that's enough.

But Nox and Azrael are missing. I hear Hellion say that we lost them but only barely, my ears ringing at the loss.

Haven's sobs cut through the room, sharp and raw. She's curled into herself in the corner, her arms wrapped tightly around her knees as if trying to hold herself together. Each sound she makes feels like a physical blow, echoing in the heavy silence of the room.

I stare at her, the weight of the words Hellion just said pressing down on me like a suffocating fog. Nox and Azrael are gone.

“No,” I whisper, shaking my head as if that could change reality. My knees feel weak, and I clutch Atlas tighter to my chest, his warmth the only thing anchoring me in this moment. "No, they can't be."

Hellion stands by the door, his face grim and pale, the fire that usually burns in his gaze dimmed to ash. "They fought until the end," he says quietly, his voice flat, as though he's forcing himself to keep it steady. "Azrael... he went after Ymir when Haven was in his grip. He didn't stand a chance against Ymir's wrath but he knew that. Nox was slammed during the tail end of the fight and Fenris was already fading just to keep Fenor alive..." He trails off, swallowing hard. "It wouldn't have mattered though, there was no saving them. They were both quick deaths."

I press a trembling hand to my mouth, my vision blurring with unshed tears. "They... they saved us all," I manage to whisper, my voice shaking. "They gave everything."

Haven's sobs intensify, her shoulders shaking violently as Vor moves to her side, placing a hand on her back. She doesn't flinch, doesn't acknowledge him, lost in her grief. I can feel her pain from across the room, a deep, guttural ache that resonates in my own chest.

Rhadis steps closer, his hand resting gently on my back. His presence is grounding, but the storm inside me doesn't settle. I glance up at him, searching his expression for something—comfort, reassurance, anything—but his face is a mask of quiet devastation.

"We'll honor them," Rhadis says softly, his voice low and steady. "Their sacrifice won't be forgotten."

I nod slowly, though the ache in my chest only deepens. Atlas shifts in my arms, his tiny whimper pulling my attention back to him. I brush a hand over his soft silver hair, the sight of him bringing a flicker of solace amidst the darkness. He doesn't understand what's happened, doesn't know the weight of the lives lost to ensure his safety and the safety of this realm. But one day, he will.

"They were our family," I murmur, my voice barely above a whisper. "Our friends. They shouldn't have—"

"Don't," Rhadis cuts me off gently, his hand tightening on my back. "Don't let guilt cloud their sacrifice. They chose to fight, Raya. They knew the risks."

Haven's cries soften to broken hiccups, and Vor whispers something to her that I can't hear. I want to go to her, to comfort her, but my legs feel like they're made of lead. Instead, I lean into Rhadis, needing his strength as much as I need to stay standing for Atlas.

Emory is deathly still on the couch where Ryat laid her, her face pale and drawn. Ryat crouches beside her, murmuring soft reassurances that I can't make out. Seeing her like this, so vulnerable, makes the reality of our losses hit even harder. We've survived—but at what cost?

"Hellion," Rhadis says, his voice cutting through the oppressive silence. "We'll need to prepare for the rites. They deserve to be honored properly."

Hellion nods stiffly, his jaw clenched. "I'll see to it."

I close my eyes, swallowing the lump in my throat as the weight of the room settles heavily on my shoulders. Nox. Azrael. Their faces flash in my mind, memories of their laughter, their strength, their unwavering loyalty. Gone. And yet, their presence lingers, a haunting reminder of what we've lost—and what we must carry forward in their names.

Ryat kneels by Emory's side, his hands trembling as he brushes a strand of silver hair from her pale face. Her chest rises and falls faintly, but her skin is cold, her expression unnaturally still. She doesn't stir, doesn't react to his touch or his whispered words.

"She's not waking up," Ryat says hoarsely, his voice thick with emotion. His dark eyes, usually so steady and sure, glisten with unshed tears. "Fenris—" He turns toward the healer still sprawled in the makeshift stretcher. "When he's stable, someone needs to—he needs to check her."

I clutch Atlas tighter against me, my arms protective around his small, fragile body as I watch the scene unfold. The grief in Ryat's voice cuts through me like a blade, and I feel my own throat tighten with the weight of it all.

"She's alive," Rhadis says, his voice firm but quiet as he steps closer to the couch where Emory lies. "Her breath is steady. Whatever this is, she's fighting."

Ryat nods sharply, his jaw clenched, but I can see the cracks forming in his resolve. He presses his forehead to Emory's hand, gripping it tightly as though willing her to respond. But the silence stretches on, and she remains motionless.

"She used everything she had," Haven whispers from her corner, her voice raw and heavy with sorrow. "She unraveled Ymir's life force, didn't she? That kind of power..." She shakes her head, unable to finish. Her tear-streaked face is turned away from us, but the anguish in her posture is unmistakable.

"Don't say that," Ryat snaps, his voice harsh as he turns to glare at her. "Don't you dare say she's—" His voice breaks, and he swallows hard, looking away. "She'll wake up. She has to. Atlas needs his mother, I need my mate."

I glance at Rhadis, whose expression is unreadable, though the weight of his emotions pulses through our bond. He's calm, composed on the surface, but I can feel the undercurrent of tension in him as he watches the scene before us.

"She'll wake," I murmur, though my own voice trembles. I step closer to the couch, my free hand resting on Ryat's shoulder.

"She's strong. Emory's always been strong."

Ryat doesn't respond, his focus entirely on Emory. He strokes her hand gently, whispering words I can't hear, his shoulders hunched and his head bowed.

Helic moves toward Fenris, who is still unconscious and pale in his stretcher, his breathing shallow. The servant works with careful precision, assessing the healer's wounds as the room remains heavy with silence.

"Fenris needs more time to recover before he can help her," Helic says softly, glancing at Rhadis. "But I'll do everything I can for both of them in the meantime."

Rhadis nods, his gaze lingering on Ryat and Emory before he turns to me. His dark eyes soften slightly, his hand brushing lightly against my arm. "You need to rest, too," he says quietly, his tone gentler than I expected. "Atlas needs you while his parents work through this."

I look down at Atlas, who has quieted in my arms but clings to me with tiny fists, his face scrunched with unease. I press a kiss to his soft hair, drawing strength from the feel of him against me.

"I'll rest once I know they're okay," I reply, my voice steady despite the storm raging inside me.

Rhadis doesn't argue, but his hand lingers on my arm, grounding me as the tension in the room thickens. We all know the battle is over, but the war isn't won—not until Emory, Fenris and Fenor open their eyes and the ones we've lost are properly mourned.

CHAPTER NINETEEN

The morning light filters weakly through the castle windows, casting pale beams onto the worn faces of everyone scattered throughout the room. The air is heavy with tension and sorrow, a quiet reminder of the toll the battle has taken on us all. I sit in a chair near Fenor's cot, Atlas nestled in my arms as I hold the small bottle to his lips. His tiny hands clutch at my fingers as he drinks, his soft breaths the only comforting sound in the otherwise hushed space.

Fenris is awake now, his breathing shallow but steady. He's propped against a mound of pillows, his face pale and gaunt. I can see the effort it takes for him to just remain conscious. Healing the others is out of the question—his body can barely keep itself alive. Helic stays nearby, monitoring him and ensuring he has water and small amounts of food to keep his strength up.

Fenor, still unconscious, looks almost as bad. His skin is far too pale, his breaths uneven, and the sight of him like this makes my chest ache. I shift Atlas in my arms, brushing a hand over his soft hair as I try to steady myself. My little nephew doesn't need to feel my grief—not when he's too young to understand what's happening around him.

I glance over at Ryat, who stands silently at the far end of the room, cradling Emory in his arms. He hasn't left her side since we got back, and the anguish in his expression is almost too much to bear. He presses his lips to her temple, whispering words I can't hear, and then turns and walks out, carrying her to their room.

Once he's gone, I turn my attention back to Fenor, shifting closer to his cot. Atlas finishes his bottle, his tiny fists clutching at my tunic as I burp him gently. I press a kiss to his soft head, drawing strength from his warmth and innocence. Once he's settled, I set the bottle aside and lean forward, brushing a hand over Fenor's damp brow.

"You're stubborn, you know that?" I murmur, my voice soft but steady. "You always have been. So you'd better fight through this, Fenor. I'm not done with you yet."

I pause, swallowing the lump in my throat as I study his too-still form. The sight of him like this—so weak, so vulnerable—stirs a mix of emotions I can barely contain. He's always been the strong one, the one who protected me no matter the cost, even if it was only as children and in these last few months. Seeing him like this feels like a cruel twist of fate.

Atlas lets out a soft coo, pulling my attention back to him. His wide, curious eyes blink up at me, and I can't help but smile, even through the pain. "Your uncle's going to be okay," I tell him, though the words are as much for myself as they are for him. "He has to be. He's too stubborn to let anything take him down."

I settle back in the chair, holding Atlas close as I continue to speak to Fenor. My words are a quiet stream, a mix of memories, reassurances, and pleas for him to wake up. The weight of the room presses down on me, but I don't stop. I can't. Talking to him feels like the only thing keeping me grounded.

The hours pass slowly, the room filled with the soft sounds of breathing and the occasional murmur from Helic as he tends to Fenris. I keep my vigil by Fenor's side, holding onto the hope that he'll wake up, that Emory will wake up, and that we can all find a way to heal from this.

Because we have to. There's no other option.

Rhadis finds me hours later, his quiet steps almost startling in the silence of the room. I've been sitting by Fenor's side, watching the shallow rise and fall of his chest, the steady rhythm of his breathing the only reassurance I have that he's still here. Atlas stirs in my arms, his tiny hand brushing my cheek as if sensing my grief.

"You need rest," Rhadis says softly, his voice steady but filled with concern. He crouches beside me, his dark eyes searching mine. "Come to sleep."

I shake my head, tightening my hold on Atlas. "I can't leave him." I whisper, my voice cracking. "What if—what if something happens?"

Rhadis places a hand on my knee, grounding me. "Helic is here.

Fenris is stable enough to monitor them. You can't carry all of this alone, Raya."

He reaches for Atlas, his movements gentle and practiced. I hesitate for a moment, but then I let him take the baby from my arms. Rhadis cradles him with the ease of someone who's been doing this for weeks, not only a day, his touch tender as he brushes a hand over Atlas's soft hair.

"Let me get him ready for bed," he says quietly. "You need to take care of yourself too."

I follow him to our room and watch as he walks to the small corner where Atlas's basket is set up, carefully dressing him in his tiny pajamas. His large hands handle the delicate buttons and soft fabric with surprising gentleness, and I can't help but feel a pang of gratitude for him—for the way he's stepped in to help with Atlas since everything fell apart.

Once Atlas is dressed and settled into his basket, his tiny breaths slow and even, Rhadis turns back to me. He takes my hand and gently pulls me to him, his strength steadying me as my legs feel weak beneath me.

"You've done enough for today," he murmurs, leading me across the room. "Let me take care of you now."

We walk to the cot, and he helps me into one of my sleep tunics, his hands brushing against my skin as he adjusts the fabric. His touch is comforting, steady, and I feel the tears welling up before I can stop them. When we lie down, he pulls me into his arms, his warmth surrounding me like a shield against the weight of everything we've lost.

"I can't stop thinking about them," I whisper, my voice trembling. "Emory, Fenor... Nox and Azrael. What if we lose them all? What if—"

Rhadis silences me with a gentle kiss to my forehead, his hand stroking my back in slow, soothing circles. "Don't," he says, his voice firm but kind. "Don't carry this burden alone. I'm here. We'll get through this together."

The dam breaks, and the tears I've been holding back spill over. I bury my face in his chest, clinging to him as the sobs wrack my body. He holds me tighter, his strength unwavering as I let myself fall apart in his arms.

"I miss them so much," I choke out, my voice muffled against his skin.

"I know," he whispers, his lips brushing against my hair. "I know, Raya. But we'll find a way. We always do."

His words are a quiet promise, a lifeline in the darkness, and as I cry myself into exhaustion, his steady presence anchors me. Eventually, the weight of my grief gives way to a fragile calm, and I drift into a restless sleep, his arms still wrapped securely around me.

CHAPTER TWENTY

The dining room feels heavy with the silence of grief. We're all here, but it's as if the air has been drained from the room. Atlas fusses in my arms as I feed him, his tiny hands gripping at my fingers as if sensing the tension surrounding us. His innocent babbling is the only sound breaking the stillness.

Across the table, Haven stares blankly at her plate, her face pale and drawn. Eira sits beside her, quietly twisting a napkin in her hands. Even Rhadis, usually so composed, leans against the back of his chair, his jaw tight with unspoken frustration. Fenris is absent, still recovering in his room, and neither Emory or Fenor have woken yet. Every glance at the empty chairs feels like a punch to the chest.

I focus on Atlas, brushing his soft hair as he takes another sip from his bottle. It's all I can do to keep from breaking apart completely.

The sound of footsteps breaks the silence. Heavy, familiar. I glance up just as Ryat enters the room, his arm wrapped tightly around Emory, who leans on him for support. My breath catches as I take in her pale face, her silver hair duller than usual. She looks fragile, as if a gust of wind could knock her over.

But she's awake. She's alive.

Everyone stirs, the chairs scraping against the floor as they rise to their feet. Emory offers a faint smile, her voice barely above a whisper as she says, "I'm okay."

Ryat guides her to a chair, helping her sit before taking the one beside her. His hand never leaves hers, and the relief on his face is palpable. "The fates sent her back," he says, his voice shaking with emotion. "She's giftless now, but she's here. She's going to be okay."

A collective gasp ripples through the room, and then chaos erupts. Haven rushes to Emory's side, tears streaming down her face as she clasps her hands. Eira and Vor exchange wide-eyed glances, while Fenor's absence is felt even more deeply in the moment.

"They took your gifts?" I ask, my voice breaking through the noise. Atlas stirs in my lap, his little fingers clutching at the fabric of my dress.

Emory nods slowly, her silver eyes meeting mine. "They said… it was the price for my actions. My gifts were tied too closely to the curse and everything it had taken from the fates. They couldn't let me keep them."

Her words hang heavily in the air, but the faint smile on her lips tells me she's made peace with it. "I'm okay with it," she says softly, her gaze flickering to Ryat. "As long as I'm here—with all of you—that's enough."

Ryat squeezes her hand, his expression fierce with determination. "You're more than enough, Emory. Always."

My throat tightens, and I shift Atlas to my other arm as I watch them. The love between them is so tangible, so overwhelming, it's impossible not to feel it. Even without her gifts, Emory shines in a way that makes me believe she'll find her strength again. She always does.

Rhadis leans forward, his voice calm but steady. "If the fates sent you back, it means your role isn't finished yet. Giftless or not, you're still one of us. And we'll protect you."

Emory nods, her eyes glistening as she looks around the room. "Thank you. All of you."

I glance down at Atlas, his soft coos a balm to the tension in my chest. The fight isn't over, not by a long shot. But as I look around the table at the people I've fought alongside, at the strength and resilience etched into every face, I feel a spark of hope reignite.

We've been through hell and back. And somehow, we're still standing. Together.

I stand, cradling Atlas in my arms as I watch Emory, her face so full of raw emotion it nearly brings tears to my eyes. Her silver hair falls messily over her shoulders, and her trembling hands reach out toward him even before I get close enough to hand him over.

"Here," I say softly, my voice catching in my throat as I settle him gently into her arms. The moment he's there, her tears fall freely.

"Oh, my sweet boy," she whispers, her voice thick with emotion as she kisses his forehead, his cheeks, his tiny hands. Each kiss seems like a silent apology, a promise, a vow all at once. Atlas squirms in her hold, his little fists opening and closing as he gurgles, his big, beautiful eyes staring up at her.

"He's perfect," Emory sobs, holding him close to her chest. "He's so perfect."

Ryat leans in beside her, placing a steadying hand on her back as he watches her with their son. His own eyes are wet, though his expression is one of fierce pride and relief. "He missed you," he murmurs, his voice breaking slightly. "I told him every day how strong his mother is. Raya watches him for me when I need a break."

Emory's gaze shifts to Ryat, her silver eyes glistening. "I missed him too," she says, her voice barely above a whisper. "I missed both of you. Thank you, Raya."

She kisses Atlas again, her lips brushing his soft hair as she begins to rock him gently. Her tears fall onto his little onesie, but she doesn't seem to notice. "You're so much bigger than I remember," she says to him, her voice breaking. "I can't believe how much time I've missed."

"You're here now," I say softly, moving to sit back down. "That's what matters."

Emory nods, pressing her cheek to Atlas's head. "I'm here now," she echoes, almost to herself. "And I'm never letting go again."

Atlas makes a happy, cooing sound, and Emory laughs through her tears. She kisses him again, her lips lingering against his chubby cheek as if she's trying to memorize the feel of him.

The room falls quiet, the weight of the moment settling over all of us. For a brief second, it's as if the war, the pain, and the losses we've endured are distant memories, and all that remains is this: a mother holding her son, a family piecing itself back together.

Ryat leans closer, brushing a kiss against Emory's temple as he rests his hand over hers, steadying her trembling grip on their child. "He loves you," Ryat murmurs. "He always knew you'd come back."

And as I sit there, watching them, I can't help but feel a flicker of hope for the first time in what feels like forever.

I sit beside Fenor's cot later that afternoon, my hand resting gently over his pale, bandaged one. His chest rises and falls steadily now, a small but significant improvement from the stillness that terrified me just days ago. Atlas is asleep in his basket by my feet, leaving me free to focus entirely on Fenor as Fenris kneels beside me, his brow furrowed in concentration.

His hands hover over Fenor's chest, faint ripples of golden light emanating from his fingers as he checks him with his dwindling powers. I feel the warmth of the magic brushing against my skin, faint but soothing. I clutch Fenor's hand a little tighter, praying silently for him to wake soon, to tell me one of his snarky jokes and make me roll my eyes.

After a long silence, Fenris inhales sharply, his eyes snapping open as he looks at me. I stiffen at his expression, my heart skipping a beat. "What is it?" I ask, my voice barely above a whisper. "What's wrong?"

Fenris doesn't respond immediately. His gaze darts between Fenor's hand, which I'm still holding, and my face. He hesitates before his lips curve into a small, knowing smile. "Raya," he says, his voice softer now, almost amused. "Since you're touching Fenor, my powers extended to you as well."

I blink, confusion and worry swirling in my chest. "And?" I ask, my throat tightening. "What did you see? Is something wrong with me?"

Fenris laughs softly, the sound full of warmth and reassurance. "No, nothing's wrong," he says, his tone light and teasing now. "In fact, you're perfectly healthy. You both are."

I frown, his words not fully sinking in. "Both?" I echo, my mind racing to catch up. "What do you mean both? Me and Fenor? Because he does not seem to be perfectly healthy."

Fenris's smile widens, and he places a comforting hand on my shoulder. "You're carrying a child, Raya," he says gently. "It's faint, but the life force is there. You're about a month in, I'd say. Maybe a little more."

The room tilts, and I feel like the air has been knocked out of me. "What?" I manage to choke out, my voice barely audible. "Are you... are you sure?"

He nods firmly, his gaze steady and certain. "Positive," he says, his tone leaving no room for doubt. "Your child is strong, just like you. Fenor will wake soon, so it seems that strength runs in your blood."

My heart pounds in my chest, a mix of disbelief, joy, and fear swirling together in a chaotic storm. I pull my hand away from Fenor's, pressing it against my flat stomach as if I might feel something, anything. "A child," I whisper, the words feeling foreign and surreal on my tongue.

Fenris chuckles again, clearly enjoying my reaction. "You'll make a good mother," he says with a wink. "And if your mate is anything like you and your brother, that child is going to have one hell of a personality."

My mind races, the reality of what he's said slowly sinking in. A child. My child. Rhadis's child. The thought is both thrilling and terrifying, and I can't help but wonder how he'll react when I tell him. Will he be as shocked as I am? Or will he already know, with that quiet, all-knowing way of his?

"Raya," Fenris says softly, pulling me from my spiraling thoughts. "You're going to be fine. Both of you. Trust me."

I nod slowly, trying to steady my breathing as I glance back at Fenor. His face is still pale, but there's color returning to his cheeks now, a small sign of life still burning within him. My fingers brush over his hand again, and I whisper, "You'll be an uncle, Fenor. You'd better wake up soon to hear the news."

Fenris smiles beside me, and though the weight of everything still feels immense, for the first time in days, I feel a flicker of hope.

I stand up and walk through the dimly lit corridors, my hand still pressed lightly against my stomach as if to anchor myself in the swirling reality of Fenris's words. A child. I repeat it in my mind, over and over, but it still feels surreal. My steps quicken as I approach Rhadis's study, needing to see him, needing to share this moment.

When I push open the heavy door, I find him sitting at his desk, folded over a thick, weathered book. His dark brows are furrowed in concentration, one hand propping up his head while the other flips a page. The dim glow of a single lantern casts shadows across his face, making him look both commanding and entirely engrossed.

"Rhadis," I call softly, stepping inside and closing the door behind me.

He glances up, his crimson-ringed eyes meeting mine, and a faint smile tugs at his lips. "Raya," he says, his voice deep and warm. "Done sharpening swords already? Or were you sitting with Fenor?"

I shake my head, taking a step closer. "No, not that. I... I needed to talk to you."

He straightens slightly, closing the book in front of him with a quiet thud. The words **Herbal Remedies for the Fatigued and Wounded** are embossed on the cover, and I realize he's been studying it to help Fenor and Fenris. My heart swells at the quiet care in his actions, and it gives me the courage to say what I need to.

"What's wrong?" he asks, concern flickering in his gaze. "Did something happen?"

I swallow hard and close the distance between us, standing beside his chair. He turns to face me fully, his hands resting on his thighs as he waits. My throat feels tight, and for a moment, I don't know how to begin. But then I take a deep breath and force the words out.

"Fenris was checking on Fenor earlier," I say, my voice trembling slightly. "And... since I was holding his hand, his powers extended to me."

Rhadis's brows draw together, his sharp gaze scanning my face as though searching for signs of illness. "What did he find?" he asks, his voice calm but edged with quiet worry.

I reach for his hand, lacing my fingers through his, and guide it to rest over my stomach. His palm is warm against me, grounding. "He found something," I say softly, my voice breaking into a nervous laugh. "Or... someone."

Rhadis's eyes widen slightly, and for a moment, he just stares at me, as if he's trying to comprehend the meaning of my words. Then, realization dawns, and his hand presses more firmly against my stomach. "You're...?" His voice is low, reverent, almost disbelieving.

I nod, tears stinging my eyes. "Yes. Fenris said "I'm about a month along."

For a moment, he's completely still, his gaze locked on my stomach as if he's trying to feel the life growing within me.

Then, slowly, his lips curl into a smile—small at first, but it grows into something that takes my breath away. His hand shifts to cup my waist, and he stands, towering over me as he pulls me into his arms.

"A child," he murmurs, his voice full of awe. "Our child."

The weight of his words sinks into me, and I feel the tears spill over, hot and unchecked. He kisses the top of my head, his grip on me firm yet gentle, as though he's afraid I might disappear if he holds me too tightly.

"I didn't know how you'd react," I admit, my voice muffled against his chest. "I was so nervous to tell you."

He pulls back just enough to look at me, his hands cupping my face. "Nervous?" he repeats, his tone both tender and teasing. "Raya, you've just given me the greatest news I could ever hear. Why would you be nervous?"

I shrug, a shaky laugh escaping me. "Because it's... a lot. Everything happening, the lives lost, the uncertainty..."

His thumbs brush away the tears on my cheeks, his gaze steady and full of unshakable confidence. "You are my mate, Raya," he says firmly. "And this child... This child is ours. There is no battle, no God, no force in this world that will take you or them from me."

The conviction in his voice makes my chest tighten, and I nod, feeling the last of my fear melt away under his unwavering gaze. "I believe you," I whisper.

He leans down, pressing his forehead against mine, his voice dropping to a low murmur. “Thank you,” he says, his breath warm against my skin. “For telling me. For carrying this gift. For being mine.”

“And you’re mine,” I reply, my voice steadier now, filled with quiet certainty.

For a long moment, we just stand there, wrapped in each other’s presence, the enormity of this new reality sinking in. Eventually, Rhadis pulls me back into his arms, his hand returning to rest over my stomach. I feel the warmth of his touch, the strength of his love, and for the first time in days, I feel truly safe. Truly at peace.

CHAPTER TWENTY-ONE

It's been a week, and the waiting has felt endless. Every day, I've sat by Fenor's side, holding his hand, speaking softly to him, hoping my voice would guide him back to us. The faint rise and fall of his chest has been the only sign of life, and though Fenris assured me he would wake, the worry has gnawed at me like an unrelenting shadow.

Today feels different. The air in the room is lighter, as though some invisible weight has been lifted. I sit beside Fenor as usual, Atlas nestled against my chest, his small breaths warm against my skin while his parents nap. I'm telling him a story, a memory of our childhood, my voice quiet so as not to disturb the silence.

"And then," I say softly, smiling down at Fenor's pale face, "you fell right into that mud pit. I think it took Mama half an hour to scrub you clean. You kept yelling that the pigs were your friends and you wanted to stay dirty with them."

Atlas gurgles softly, his little hands grasping at the edge of my shirt, and I chuckle. "You'd have loved to see that, little one. Your uncle was always finding ways to get into trouble."

As I speak, something shifts. I feel it before I see it—a faint tightening of Fenor's hand beneath mine. My heart leaps, and I lean closer, my breath catching as his fingers twitch again.

"Fenor?" I whisper, my voice trembling. "Can you hear me?"

His eyelids flutter, and a low, raspy groan escapes him. Tears blur my vision as I watch him struggle, his body weak but alive, pushing against the haze that's kept him under for so long. His green and brown eyes crack open, unfocused at first, but slowly sharpening as they find mine.

"Raya," he croaks, his voice hoarse and barely audible. "What... happened?"

A sob escapes me, and I squeeze his hand tightly, unable to hold back my tears. "You're awake," I manage to say, my voice breaking. "You're here. You're okay."

His gaze flickers to Atlas, who coos softly, and a faint smile touches his cracked lips. "Is that... Emory's boy?"

I nod quickly, tears streaming down my face as I cradle Atlas closer. "Yes, it's Atlas. He's been keeping me company while I wait for you to wake up."

Fenor's smile grows, though it's weak, and he shifts slightly on the cot, wincing at the effort. "Feels like... I've been gone forever."

I shake my head, brushing his hair back from his forehead, my touch trembling. "It doesn't matter how long, Fenor. You're back now. That's all that matters."

The door creaks open, and Fenris steps inside, his weary eyes widening as he takes in the scene. Relief floods his expression, and he crosses the room in a few quick strides, his hands glowing faintly as he places them on Fenor's chest.

"You're awake," Fenris murmurs, his voice filled with wonder. "Thank the Gods."

Fenor's gaze flickers to him, and a faint smirk tugs at his lips. "Missed me, didn't you?"

Fenris laughs, though it's shaky, and he shakes his head. "You've no idea. Let me check you over. Don't move too much."

Fenris's powers sweep over Fenor, the glow pulsing softly as he works. Atlas begins to fuss in my arms, and I rock him gently, whispering soothing words as I watch my brother. Fenris's expression grows lighter, and he finally steps back, nodding in satisfaction.

"You're stable," he says, his voice filled with relief. "Weak, but stable. You'll need rest, but you'll recover."

Fenor's eyes close briefly, as though the effort of staying awake is already too much, but when he opens them again, they're fixed on me. "Raya," he murmurs. "Thank you… for staying."

My throat tightens, and I nod, brushing more tears from my cheeks. "Always," I whisper. "I'll always stay."

Fenris squeezes my shoulder gently before stepping back, giving us space. I cradle Atlas closer, my heart full as I watch Fenor drift back into a peaceful sleep. He's alive. He's here. And for the first time in what feels like an eternity, hope blooms in my chest again.

CHAPTER TWENTY-TWO

The clearing is quiet, save for the soft rustling of leaves in the cool breeze. The entire group is gathered, dressed in dark shades, the weight of loss heavy in the air. The pyres are set, two in the center of the clearing, with flowers and tokens of love carefully placed around them. The scent of rosemary and sage lingers, their smoke curling into the gray sky above.

I stand beside Rhadis, his hand a steadying presence on my back as I watch Arden with Atlas. His bright curiosity feels out of place in this solemn moment. He doesn't understand what this is, what we've all endured to stand here today.

Fenor is beside me, pale and still recovering, but strong enough to stand through this final rite. His hand brushes mine, a quiet reminder of his support. I glance at him briefly, my heart swelling with relief that he's still here, even as we grieve those we've lost.

The priestess steps forward, her soft voice rising as she begins the ceremony. "Today, we honor the lives of Azrael and Nox, brave warriors who gave everything to protect this realm. Their sacrifices will not be forgotten, and their names will live on in the hearts of those they loved."

The words sting, a sharp ache in my chest, but I force myself to stay strong. I glance across the circle, seeing Haven standing alone. Her arms are wrapped around herself, her once fierce and confident presence now shattered. The light in her eyes is dim, and her shoulders sag under the weight of grief. She stares at the pyres, unmoving, her face pale and hollow.

I wish I could do something—say something to ease her pain—but I know nothing I offer will mend her broken heart. Azrael's death has taken a piece of her, a piece she may never recover.

The priestess's voice continues, steady and soothing. "We commit their spirits to the stars, where they may watch over us and guide us in our darkest hours. Let us carry their strength and courage with us, always."

Ryat steps forward, his expression solemn, Emory beside him holding his arm for support. She's pale, her body still weak, but she stands tall as Ryat lights the first pyre. The flames catch quickly, consuming the wood and beginning to lick at the tokens of remembrance.

Emory's soft words break through the quiet. "Thank you," she says, her voice trembling but firm. "For everything."

I tighten my hold on Rhadis, my throat tightening as the second pyre is lit. The flames leap high, crackling and snapping as they devour the wood. The smoke curls upward, carrying with it the memories, the sacrifices, the essence of those we've lost.

Haven doesn't move. She doesn't cry or speak. She simply watches, her eyes fixed on the flames as though searching for something she'll never find. Her grief is palpable, a heavy cloud that presses against my chest.

When the flames begin to settle, Rhadis leans down, his lips brushing my ear. "Are you all right?"

I nod, though the lump in my throat makes it hard to speak. "It's just… so final," I whisper, my voice barely audible.

He wraps an arm around me, his warmth a small comfort against the chill in the air. I glance back at Atlas, his little face serene as he drifts off to sleep against Ardens chest. I wonder what kind of world we'll build for him now—one without Azrael and Nox, one where their sacrifices mean something.

The priestess steps back, her voice soft as she concludes. "Let us honor them with the lives we live, with the love we share, and the courage we carry. May their spirits find peace within the Underworld."

The group stands in silence for a moment, the only sound the crackling of the dying flames. Then, slowly, people begin to move. Ryat leads Emory away, his hand steady on her back. Fenris helps Fenor to a nearby bench, his own exhaustion evident.

I hesitate, glancing back at Haven. She hasn't moved, her eyes still fixed on the pyres.

“Haven,” I say softly, stepping toward her. “Do you want to come inside?”

She doesn’t respond at first, her expression blank. Then, finally, she shakes her head, her voice barely above a whisper. “Not yet.”

I want to pull her into a hug, to give her some of the strength she’s lost, but I know she isn’t ready. Instead, I nod, giving her space, and turn back to Rhadis, who is waiting for me with a quiet patience.

As we walk back toward the castle, I can’t help but glance up at the sky. The stars aren’t visible yet, but I like to think Azrael and Nox are already up there, watching over us. They gave their lives so we could have this moment, so we could keep moving forward.

I lean into Rhadis’s side, his strength grounding me as we make our way inside. There’s so much still to heal, so many scars that will never fully fade, but we’re here. Together. And for now, that’s enough.

About The Author

Born in the small town of Keosauqua, Iowa, Kay Hughes spent the first twelve years of her life traveling the United States with her parents and younger brother, an experience that inspired her boundless imagination. Specializing in Fantasy Romance, Kay crafts vivid worlds filled with epic battles, enchanting magic and unforgettable love stories. When not writing, Kay enjoys crocheting, reading, and swimming with her three beloved dogs.

Made in the USA
Monee, IL
02 August 2025

21858703R00142